Home Always Beckons

Lana Lynne

Home Always Beckons

A New Sunrise

Judy,
May You Always Find
Your Way Home!
Blessings,
Lana Lynne

TATE PUBLISHING *& Enterprises*

Home Always Beckons
Copyright © 2009 by Lana Lynne. All rights reserved.

No part of this publication may be reproduced, stored in a retrieval system or transmitted in any way by any means, electronic, mechanical, photocopy, recording or otherwise without the prior permission of the author except as provided by USA copyright law.

Scripture quotations are taken from the *Holy Bible, King James Version,* Cambridge, 1769. Used by permission. All rights reserved.

The opinions expressed by the author are not necessarily those of Tate Publishing, LLC.

Published by Tate Publishing & Enterprises, LLC
127 E. Trade Center Terrace | Mustang, Oklahoma 73064 USA
1.888.361.9473 | www.tatepublishing.com

Tate Publishing is committed to excellence in the publishing industry. The company reflects the philosophy established by the founders, based on Psalm 68:11,
"The Lord gave the word and great was the company of those who published it."

Book design copyright © 2009 by Tate Publishing, LLC. All rights reserved.
Cover design by Lance Waldrop
Interior design by Stefanie Rooney

Published in the United States of America

ISBN: 978-1-60696-535-1
1. Fiction, Romance, Historical
2. Juvenile Fiction, Historical, United States, Civil War
09.02.23

Dedicated
to
my parents and grandparents
and
in honor of
my great-grandparents, who lived and
served during the Civil War

~

In memory of my mother

Author's Note and Acknowledgments

Home Always Beckons is a work of historical fiction. All characters are fictional except those who are historically known, i.e., Abraham Lincoln, General Frederick Steele, General Hood, the Pierce brothers. I have tried to weave real situations occurring historically at this time into the fictional lives and situations needed for telling the stories of my characters. Rockport, Arkansas, has a rich history during this period. Two historical events of real townspeople are mentioned in chapter three: the "Arkansas Drum Maker" and violin player, Henry Clay Ward, and the shooting of the town doctor's five-year-old son by a Union soldier. I gratefully acknowledge the help with my research of Rockport completed by my late Aunt Azalee Duke of Arkadelphia, Arkansas, and by Brenda Matthews of the Malvern Chamber of Commerce. Any errors or adjustments made regarding historical events in order to develop this work of fiction are my own. There is a list of research sources provided at the end of the book. I hope this encourages many to learn more about this tragic but inspiring time in history. The resilience of the people, both north and south, who survived the horrible war and became the United States of America is an inspiration to all of us.

~ Lana Lynne ~

Chapter One

The stars glistened throughout the Arkansas night sky as the three men rode into town. There were only the sounds of crickets singing and shouts of laughter from the town saloon to greet them. The stable at the end of the street became clearer as the men approached it.

As they dismounted, a short, dumpy man emerged from the livery stable, his swift eyes appraising the newcomers as well as their horses.

"What kind of horses are them? Kinda small ain't they?" he greeted.

He swallowed hard as the three men stepped into the pool of light offered by the lantern beside the stable door; they all stood at least six feet and were muscled by years of outside labor.

He began to stammer slightly.

"I do-don't mean no offense. I just never seen … What can I do for you fellows?"

The men exchanged glances and then grinned.

Dark brown hair was revealed as the middle

one stepped forward, taking off his dusty hat as he stretched his angular, tightly-toned form.

"They're Texas mustangs. They may be small, but they get the job done when you're herding cattle. I'm Marcus Johnson."

He extended his hand.

It was received by the broad one of Sam Owens.

"Sam Owens. I own this here livery. So, you from Texas?"

Marcus gathered the reins of their mounts and handed them to Mr. Owens.

"Only Boyd Richards here." He motioned to the burnished, golden-haired man on his right. "John and I are from some farms not far from Rockport."

The older man smiled at Marcus before taking a closer look at his companions. Marc noticed the man's gaze didn't rest long on Boyd, who had favored the poor man with a cold, empty gaze. Instead, it quickly shifted to the characteristically warm, slow smile of John.

"Well, welcome back. You boys should be home by tomorrow 'bout supper time. You're welcome to spread your bedrolls in that empty stall yonder. Things sure changed at Rockport when General Steele brought his federal troops there during the war. My cousin lives there, and he says they're just now starting to finish the courthouse; but the river trade is really picking up on the Ouachita again."

Sam had helped remove the men's gear, saddles, and bridles from their ponies as he spoke. Marc

for more information or to place an order, contact:
TATE PUBLISHING & Enterprises
www.tatepublishing.com/bookstore
888.361.9473

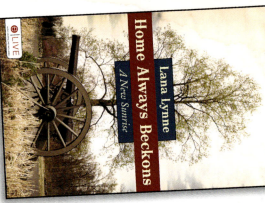

Home Always Beckons

Marcus Johnson and John Wilkins marched from Rockport, Arkansas, over five years ago to aid in resolving the war that divided the nation. Many friends and family members fought beside them. Some returned home, spent and broken. Others remained where they had fallen, leaving only memories for their families. John and Marc had made a rare choice. They would not make the return journey for a time.

They had found solace after the war in work with Texas cattlemen. Now the devastation they discover in their home state further deepens the waters of guilt that engulf them as they ultimately travel home to Rockport. The Civil War had painfully reached the very doors of the family and friends they had left behind. Anger, forgiveness, betrayal, and love are waiting for them.

Faces and names echo from the trees and farms. But when John and Marc discover romance in the surprising love of two sisters, a new sunrise dawns.

accepted his offer for lodging, and they settled in for the night.

Marc lay on the blanket roll padded by hay underneath and reflected on all the changes the Civil War had forced on all their lives. It had been two years since it ended, and this was the first time John and he had been home. There had been so many changes within him to face during the aftermath. He refused to go home and face the changes the war had worked and the bitter ones now being forced due to Reconstruction. However, the latter had now brought him and his friends to face scarred land and the families who had weathered violent conflict. He had received a letter from his mother. A lump formed in his throat as he recalled more what was left unsaid as said in the gentle slope of words.

Dear Son,

I hope this letter finds you well. We are all in good health, but our hearts are pricked daily by the news of our government's struggles with this new presidential Reconstruction period. Your Pa is making as much out of the farm as he can for us. We love you and hope you're finding enough work. I understand your reluctance to come home, but know we do miss you. God bless.

Love,
Ma

Marc sighed deeply. It was past time he came home. Sleep came slowly as he tried to mentally rehearse how his homecoming would actually be. He had many different versions when he had considered coming home during the past years. Tomorrow those daydreams would become real. He slept peacefully as the whippoorwill lulled him to sleep.

The next morning Marc rose early to the sound of cows and horses. He quickly rolled his blanket, found his boots, and began to saddle his horse. John Wilkins, his best friend since childhood, walked in the livery door as he finished. Taking the reins in his hand, he went to meet him with his horse trailing behind him.

"Morning, John. You ready?"

He met the serious, brown eyes, which quickly met his, paused, and then looked away. John was the peacemaker, the quiet agreeable type. Marc had known there would be a limit to his friend's endless patience one day. This was the day. His tall, broadshouldered friend ducked his head, kicking at the ground in a gesture very familiar to Marcus. It meant John Wilkins was finding it hard to speak because his words might cause conflict.

The voice was deep with attempts to conceal emotions.

"Yeah, I don't know how we could have stayed away for over five years. I know the first four weren't our choice, the war, but the past almost year and a half…" His voice trailed off as he shook his head in disbelief, and telling moisture glimmered in his eyes. "How? Everyone else left in our regiment went home: my pa, Richard, and his pa. I know they weren't taken prisoner like we were, but how did we stay away—"

"This long?" Marc finished for his friend. "Self-ishness, guilt, take your pick. If we had waited a few more months, it would have been six years. Why didn't we wait another year? Then it would have been closer to seven years. Isn't there something in the Bible about debts being forgiven after seven years? Maybe we could have been forgiven that way... it's time to stop! We have made many errors in judgment. It's time to let go of the bitterness. Let's go home."

He briefly squeezed John's shoulder, side-stepped agilely and continued out the door with his horse.

Boyd Richards was waiting astride his mustang outside the stable door as Marc emerged.

He tipped his hat back, revealing a direct amber gaze. His Georgian-turned-Texan drawl was sardonic as he said, "If I overheard you right, I'm not throwing in with y'all about letting go of the bitterness. It's the only emotion I'm sure I can still feel. I think I'll keep it." He nodded toward John as he joined them. "Yet I would agree it's time to get you boys home."

The men urged their horses forward.

As they rode, there were scattered signs of the destitution and post-war suffering which had been described in the letters from home that had reached them. The Reconstruction, which had started in 1865, looked to be going slowly. It was now October of 1866.

Autumn. Marc stopped pondering the changes and instead began to enjoy the scenic, rural things that were enduring: the beautiful trees, which were tall and thick with leaves of varied hues, the smell of the close-by Ouachita River, and the land. Marc thought of his family's farm and urged his horse into a quicker pace. The other two men shared a glance and then matched the new pace.

The Wilkins' farmhouse was gray and lonely-looking as the threesome approached. A small woman came out of the house at the sound of horses. Her eyes were arrested by the sight of the black-haired man in the middle. Ever since they had received John's letter, her heart had skipped a beat each time she heard hoof beats, hoping it was him. She ran slightly forward as the three dismounted.

"John!" she exclaimed, throwing herself into her son's arms.

"Ma!" He hugged her closely, the years rolling away to his boyhood. He stepped back slightly, and rising emotions roughened his voice as he asked, "Where's Pa?"

Mary Wilkins looked up at her twenty-five-year-old son, his dark hair and eyes, so like her own, in wonderment. He had become a gentle giant of a man. Gone was the awkward, gangly youth who had openly displayed his slow, shy grin as he had marched beside his younger brother that day so long ago. Grief overcame her heart for a moment. Then, glancing over his shoulder, she recovered herself. She recognized the man on the left as Marcus Johnson, their closest neighbor's son; the other somber one she did not know. She glanced back to her son.

"Your Pa is over at the Johnson's helping with a sick cow." She now pushed him back slightly and stepped forward. "Have you forgotten your manners? Introduce me."

"Ma, this is Boyd Richards. We met him during the war when our regiment joined with Hood's Texas brigade, and then after the war we all worked in Texas on the cattle ranch I wrote you about."

"Ma'am." Boyd tipped his hat.

"And you know Marc."

Mary gazed at the chestnut-haired man she had seen shadow her son in the now past childhood years and sighed. She had shared tears with Emily Johnson often during the absence of their sons as they shared the agonies of mothers who needed to touch their sons after the end of a tragedy to be sure that they are truly all right. Emily had always apologized, saying at least Marc was alive. Yes, she knew John was alive too, but her arms had ached doubly; her other son had been killed at Chickamauga in September 1863. Her husband had returned uninjured, but her family had been incomplete. To totally lose Matthew and not see John for all these years, she shook her head and approached Marcus.

"Marcus Johnson, I am truly glad to see you, but I will not be the first to hug you this day. That is for your mother. You climb right back on that horse and go home."

Marc quickly complied.

"Yes, ma'am."

She turned back to Boyd.

"Mr. Richards, Would you be so kind as to accompany Marc and return with my husband? I am very much looking forward to having you stay with us." She glanced at John. "My house will feel more complete now you and John are here."

John saw the brief pain of loss fill his mother's, as well as Boyd's, eyes as she spoke. He moved to stand behind her with his hands on her shoulders. His eyes communicated with both Boyd and Marc. They nodded and quickly left.

Boyd glanced sideways at Marc as they rode, noting the tremor in his jaw, which always meant the younger man was clinching his jaw while in deep thought. The past two years had taught him that silence was best at moments like these. He would wait for his friend to speak. His gaze shifted back to the dirt road and countryside before him. He reflected on the scene of John and his mother reuniting and felt his chest constrict. There had been no homecoming for him. The one certainty he knew was how much he would give to have a family who was there for him. He had gone home, but all that had been home was gone.

"Boyd! Boyd!"

He heard his companion's voice pulling him back to the present.

"Yeah, Marc?"

He followed the pointing finger of the man by

his side to a farm that was not so different than the Wilkins farm, only slightly larger. He could see people by the barn.

He watched Marc slowly dismount, take his hat off, and release the breath he had been holding for the last few moments. Marc glanced up at Boyd and motioned for him to also leave his saddled position.

"I need to walk the rest of the way. It's hard to explain, but this is the longest part of the journey so far."

Green eyes implored tawny golden eyes to understand. They did. Both men knocked some of the dust off their clothes and then moved unhurriedly along the dirt road to the farm yard. One savoring all aspects of once again walking on the soil where he had taken his first steps, smelling the aroma of the ground, which had yielded harvests, and seeing the distant shapes of people who held the vestige of a family he longed to embrace. The other was apprehensively filled with happiness for his friend yet not wanting to have to torturously observe another homecoming that could never be his.

Lee Johnson and Carl Wilkins had advanced from their places by the barn to meet the approaching figures. They had soberly been discussing the chances of the cow to which they had been tending when the sound of horses snorting and the sight of two walking men distracted them.

"I wonder if one of their horses is limping," said the hazel-eyed, dark-haired man with scattered graying strands throughout.

"No. Don't appear to be," said the taller, green-eyed man with deep chestnut hair and a tanned face weathered by years of farm work. "I don't...Wait, Carl."

Lee Johnson's eyes scrutinized the darker of the two progressing visitors. Never a man for outwardly showing deep emotions, the reality that the son he had last seen walking away as a farm boy was now returning as a twenty-four-year-old man created an inward struggle of great magnitude. He and his younger sons had been ill that June when the Third Arkansas Infantry Regiment, Company F, left Rockport. He thought he would join the fighting later, and yet, as events occurred, he never had.

He took long purposeful strides to meet his oldest son with his hand outstretched. He saw strong emotions displayed on Marc's face before the young man dropped the reins of his horse and clasped the callused, large hand.

"Son."

Gazes locked and words were not needed. The joined hands bridged the years, and the strength of father and son gave mutual support. "You will want to see your mother."

"Yes, sir."

Lee saw Marc's eyes travel to Carl Wilkins, who was anxiously scanning the horizon behind them.

"John is at home. Mrs. Wilkins asked that Boyd here come and get you. Pa, Mr. Wilkins, meet my friend, Boyd Richards," Marcus said.

"Richards."

Handshakes were given, and then Boyd and Carl left. Carl was questioning Boyd about Texas and John as they walked away.

The two remaining men turned toward the house. Inside, a tall, still slim woman of forty years stood rolling out a pie crust on a long wood table. Her shoulders were slightly hunched forward as she worked at this task. She paused to push a tendril of hair away. The sound of footsteps did not alarm her; she was used to her two youngest sons running in and out many times a day. Therefore, she did not turn, nor did she waste a gaze to see who it was.

"Jack? Will? You've been gone to the Cushmans' too long. Your pa will skin you alive. He had to go get Mr. Wilkins to help him with that cow 'cause you weren't back."

Marcus was touched by the sight of the woman who had given birth to him, the light brown hair pulled into a knot at the nape of her neck with escaping curls that would not be restrained. She used to threaten to cut it off and be done with trying to contain it. Marc smiled and slowly crossed the room to stand beside her. He reached a hand to still the rolling pin that had resumed its work. Long, slender fingers reached to cover the large, tanned hand. A mother memorizes every inch and mannerism of her children. Emily Johnson closed her eyes as they filled with tears, and her hand covered that of her firstborn. Twin streams coursed down her face as she allowed her blue-green gaze to travel from the hand, up the arm, and into the face of the son she felt may never return to her.

"Thank the Lord," she exclaimed and was gathered into strong arms.

The years of having an empty place in their home were over. Marc had finally come home. She had prayed and waited, knowing her son had felt he could not come home right after the war. This knowledge did not help her understand why, but she knew that he must work it out in his time. None of that seemed to matter now. She buried her face in his shirt and wept tears of joy.

Marc felt her tears wet the shoulder of his shirt and tightened his arm protectively around her. Guilt and remorse filled him. His father moved into his line of vision as he moved to the fireplace to get his pipe from its place on the mantel. A paternal look urged him to speak.

"Ma, I am sorry."

He gave no excuses; there were none that mattered at this moment. He gently shifted her away from him to look into her face. There were changes of time as well as the work of deep-felt sorrow from the years he had held himself apart from home. However, there was also a deeper strength bred from faith exercised during a time of trial. His parent's faith had carried them through many difficulties. He could see it still did.

She shook her head.

"I'll have none of that. You are here now. What's been is over. Now, let me look at you." She held him slightly away from her. "Just as I thought. You need a good meal."

She broke away and pushed him toward the table. Marc joined his father, who was now sitting at the table smoking his pipe. His mother hurriedly placed a cup of coffee on the table and then busied herself preparing his plate of food. He sighed, beginning to feel himself relax a little, and shared a smile with his father. Suddenly he realized that there was something, no, two somebodies missing.

"Pa, did Ma say that Jack and Will are at the Cushmans'?" he inquired, his curiosity getting the best of him. Only a special event would cause his young brothers to be gone during the work day.

Lee Johnson smiled broadly.

"That's right. The charms of Alice Cushman are great motivations to finish chores early." He chuckled at the look of surprise displayed on his eldest son's face. "Son, your brothers are fifteen and seventeen now."

Surprise turned into an expression of total incredulousness.

"I guess the fact that they would be older was there in my mind, but … " He shook his head. "So, I guess everyone grew up, not just me. How old are the Cushmans' children?"

He remembered being pursued by Dawn Cushman. She had been a pretty little blonde-haired young woman of fifteen when he left.

His father broke his thoughts.

"Well, let's see. Richard's your age: twenty-four.

He married shortly after he returned from the war." There was a pause of regret. Lee continued, not looking at his son, "Dawn's twenty, Florence is eighteen, and Alice is fifteen."

Marc clasped both hands together and leaned forward on the table.

"Are Dawn and Florence married?" Florence had been the tag-a-long during his, Richard, Matt, and John's fishing trips. Dawn had preferred to sew and bake with her Ma. Her skin had been fair and smooth, while Florence's was speckled with brown sugar freckles across her nose. They both had well attained the age to marry. Marc had considered Dawn at one time before the war. He looked up to find his pa shaking his head.

"No. The war changed the number of young men to come calling. However, I heard tell of a few of our returning soldiers bringing home wives they met during the war from other states. Jack McRae found his wife in Alabama. She lived on one of those big plantations. Her family did not approve of her marrying a simple blacksmith and moving here. They have been happy, though." He quickly glanced at his wife, who was retrieving sweet potatoes from the coals in the fireplace. "Emily, we will go fetch the boys and be back for supper shortly."

He gestured to Marc and headed for the door. Marc stood and quickly gave his ma another hug before running to catch up to the elder man, the man who was now more than halfway across the field behind their house.

Chapter
Two

Grasshoppers danced in flight across Florence's path as she made her way to the special grouping of trees. She smiled at the synchrony of movement that occurred so naturally.

These trees had been her haven throughout her childhood. The overhanging branches transported her into their shaded shadows, and she sighed peacefully, making her way to the seat of roots emerging from "her special tree." As she settled against the solid trunk, her eyes drank in the lovely landscapes of which she had the perfect vantage point. Rolling pastures now browning as the seasons changed, a tranquil pond, and varied trees highlighted by golden and copper hues. She pulled her knees beneath her chin and gazed thoughtfully at this land she loved. Random leaves spiraled lazily to the ground. Tilting her head sideways with an upward glance, she uttered a prayer of thankfulness. During the war, her parents would not allow her to walk alone or far from the house. They still were guarded due to all the strangers passing through as, what was the word, yes, Reconstruction was occurring. Today there had been so much activity at home with the Johnson boys visiting that they had readily agreed to let her go for a walk.

The storm clouds that had been in the distance were moving closer, and the curtain of rain could be seen slowly advancing toward her. Her first inclination was to run to the house, yet instead she relaxed and waited for the refreshing shower. The air smelled of the impending wetness, and her nostrils were filled with the wonderful aroma. Droplets fell through the leaves, cooling her skin, running down her nose, and plastering her hair to her scalp. A smile danced about her mouth. She had never felt so relaxed.

"Florence."

A youthful male voice interrupted her solitude from a distance. She tensed. That voice, a tinge of whining to it, had irritated her for years. Arnold Beasley, the carrot-haired, speckle-faced, puppy-eyed shadow that now disturbed her. He had been adamantly pursuing her lately. She closed her eyes tightly, willing him to go away.

"There you are, Florence," he said, frowning as he reached her. "You really should start wearing your hair up. After all, you are no longer a school girl. You are a young woman and need to act accordingly."

"Arnold, why are you here?"

She stood up, angrily pushing her now damp mass of long copper hair out of her smoldering gray eyes. She dusted a few leaves from her skirt as she stepped forward to meet him. She did not have far to look up to meet his eyes. Arnold was only a couple of inches taller than her. He was short and had a stocky build. He wasn't fat, just solid, yet still had the awkwardness from incomplete adjustment into his maturing frame.

"I stopped by your house, and your pa told me you were walking. He asked me to come get you because—"

He was cut off as Florence steamed, "Because it rained? I have done this before."

Arnold shook his head. "No, because you have company."

Florence was puzzled. "Company? Will and Jack aren't company."

Arnold was shaking his head.

"Who then?"

A smirk crossed the heavily-freckled male face. He looked like a barn cat that had just had a mouse. Florence could not imagine who could be so important a visitor as to cause this much excitement.

Arnold turned and started through the trees. Florence hurried to catch up with him.

"Who is it?"

He began to hum and strode purposefully across the pasture, enjoying the feeling of her following him for a change.

"Arnold Beasley, you tell me who is at my house this instant!"

He started to run, and she stayed at his heels. They rounded the corner of the house. Arnold slowed

HOME ALWAYS BECKONS ~ 25

to a walk. Florence continued to question him loudly. They were beside the tall front porch. She could hear voices.

Before she could round the last corner and look up to see who was seated there, Alice, her younger sister, flanked on either side by Will Johnson and Jack Johnson, leaned over the wooden side rail.

"Florence, you will never believe who has come home."

The pretty, round face with dancing dove eyes was smiling widely.

She quickly turned the corner and mounted the eight steps to the top of the porch. Her older sister, Dawn Cushman, was seated in a chair opposite of…could it be? Marcus Johnson? She thought he was grown when he left, but now he was, well, a man. He looked up from his conversation with her eldest sister as she stepped onto the wooden-planked landing in front of him. He shifted toward her, crossed his arms, and leaned back slightly in his chair as his eyes completed a quick but detailed perusal of her. She defiantly flipped her rain-darkened hair over her shoulders and wiped off a streak of dirt from her nose. He seemed to be trying to distinguish the little girl from the emerging young woman before him.

She saw him glance at the young man who had followed her up the steps.

"Arnold, are you sure this is the one you want to call on? She still looks like my fishing buddy to me."

Marc's river green eyes sparkled as he received the expected glare from the subject of his comment.

It quickly turned into a smile as she said, "Same old Marc." She moved over to sit by her Ma on the bench near the door. She cocked her head to the side. "I'm glad."

He turned toward his brothers and Alice as he ran a hand through his chestnut brown hair. She watched as he contemplatively stroked his mustached lip and knew he was closing himself off from her for some reason. The Marcus she had known had been adventurous and sure of himself. He had always won all the races at school and had learned to break wild horses from her sister-in-law's father shortly before the war. Her older brother, Richard, had tried to be like him. All the girls had favored his daring spirit, especially her sister Dawn. She pulled her short legs up under her dress, laying her head on her knees as she studied her taller older sister and wondered if those fond feelings remained. Marc's rich, smooth voice shook her from her troublesome thoughts, and she turned to listen as he talked to her younger sister.

"Now, Alice," Marc said, looking at the trio, "which one of my brothers do you favor more?"

Alice blushed. "I'm not saying."

The two young men exchanged mischievous grins.

"Aw, come on, Alice. You know you like me the best," whined Jack, the younger one.

"No, she likes me best. Don't ya, Alice?" prompted Will.

Alice looked heavenward. "You two are impossible!" she wailed.

Everyone laughed.

Arnold sat on the top step. "Excuse me, Marc. Have you really been in Texas for working on two years now?"

Marc shifted his focus to the eager young man. He saw the longing for adventure and anticipation of excitement on the face of one who had not, fortunately, learned the realities of the adult world. He also realized the questions were now beginning and was thankful they concerned his post-war period. He leaned back slightly in his chair and quickly scanned the inquisitive faces surrounding him. The muscle in his clinched jaw began to twitch as he leaned forward, elbows on knees, head down momentarily, before looking up to begin relating the events of the past year and four months.

"Yes, well, actually, we—John, Boyd, and I—started out in Virginia. We had been transferred to City Point after being held prisoners at Ft. Delaware. We were captured at Gettysburg. We thought we would go to David's Island with some of the others of our company. John and I were too weak to travel on foot, so Boyd was able to get us a wagon ride. Let's just say there were a few people willing to help. We made it to Mississippi and then into Louisiana. Boyd was trying to get home and take care of us. I was better by that time, but John... Anyway, as we traveled, we heard rumors that Texas had too many cattle due to the cattlemen having left their herds to go wild while they were away fighting. There were too many to handle within the state. The prices dropped, and the cattlemen had to kill many herds. The only money was in hides and tallow. As you know, the South's post-war state promised poverty. So when we heard that two brothers, Jonathan and Abel Pierce, in Texas were doing this and were looking for hands, Boyd agreed to get us to South Texas. However, it was under the condition that we stop for a time at his home in the eastern part of the state." He paused, contemplating whether to elaborate, and decided against it. Those were matters for Boyd to share if and when he decided to do so. He continued. "Let's just say Boyd did not end up needing more than a few hours at home. We found the Pierces and began work. The New Orleans market increased as the herds became smaller. The Matagordian steers are strong. When we left, they were planning the trail to Kansas."

He looked up as his father cleared his throat.

Lee Johnson was a man of few words. Marc knew it was time for discussion of the past to stop for now.

His father rose and turned to Ella Cushman to say, "Thank you for tolerating my younger sons today and for sharing your porch this late in the day. Emily will be fretting if we don't get to supper." Lee turned to Alan Cushman. "I'll save you the trouble of having to run the boys off with a shotgun. Will, Jack, it's time we get home. Good evening, Alice, Flor-

HOME ALWAYS BECKONS ~ 29

ence, Dawn," and as he made his way down the steps, "Arnold."

Marc appreciated the fact that his father had not ordered him like his brothers. He was being treated as an adult who knew protocol. He tipped his hat and nodded to the gathered group. He paused in front of Dawn. "I'll see you in a couple of days. Maybe John and Boyd can come then."

Dawn nodded. "I will be looking forward to it." As he started down the steps, she added, "Marcus, tell your Pa that Will and Jack did help my pa with some barn repairs today."

Marc grinned. "He won't believe it." He glanced at Alice, who blushed furiously. Shaking his head, he continued down the steps and started across the yard.

He heard uneven, heavy footfalls behind him and turned. Alan Cushman stopped in front of him. Smoky gray eyes, always direct and open, halted any words Marc might have been about to say. The tension and emotion crackled. Mr. Cushman had left for the war with Carl, John, Marc, and Richard, his son. He had returned after a year with a shattered knee and dysentery.

"Marcus, I just wanted you to know, I understand why you didn't come home. I had to; there were people here who were counting on me. The things I saw and experienced during that year..." Mr. Cushman looked down and then slowly back to view Marc's face, which was teeming with varied emotions.

"Thank you, sir, but I don't understand now that

I'm here. That first year was rough, but you have no idea, begging your pardon, sir, about the ones that followed. Being taken prisoner and then being at Ft. Delaware, I can't even talk about it now."

Marc anxiously tried to gage whether he had offended this man whom he respected so much.

Images of men depleted by scurvy, many too weak to walk, overtook his mind. The dampness, the cold, the mosquitoes, the hopelessness that was the atmosphere of prison life came back to haunt him. The battlefields had been a nightmare, but at least you were free and had hope for victory. He closed his eyes tightly, shook his head, and took in a haggard breath. Opening his eyes, he encountered the ashen face of the man who had fought beside him in the field until a Minié ball bullet exploded into his right leg. While in the field hospital, they all thought he would lose his leg. Marc had been relieved to receive a letter from his mother, once Mr. Cushman had been discharged home, that he had kept his leg. However, Alan had been unable to return to the fighting.

The older man's face went from gray to a bit flush before he spoke.

"Marc, I am sorry. There is no denying the fact that no one who was not in your place can truly understand, but I can come closer to understanding you as well as the people who were here. You were in the horror of the places away from here. There were hardships here as well. When you are ready to hear about them, I'll talk, because you won't hear it from your family or John's family." He paused, saw the impact of his words register, and felt the flash of anger leave him. He had wanted to be someone Marc could talk to about all the pent-up memories and emotions. Marc's father had been able to remain at home during the war and would be unable to picture the memories of war that were harbored within the young man's brain. Old fathering habits had crept in; he never could abide when his children thought there was no one who could understand what they were feeling. He reached over and patted Marc on the shoulder.

"Just know that I am here, comrade, neighbor."

Marc was shaken and humbled. "Thank you, sir. Thank you," he said and then paused. "What about Richard? Will he talk to me?"

Alan Cushman had to choose his words carefully. His son, Richard, had suffered illnesses and wounds and yet had returned home at the war's end ready to help their community be restored. They had spoken of Marc and John many times. Richard had held the fifteen-year-old hand of John's brother, Matt, as his life bled away at Chickamauga. John had been a prisoner for two months at that time. Alan ran a hand through his hair and fixed his gaze on Marc.

"He is very resentful of you at this point. You will have to go to him yourself."

Marc hung his head, nodded, then strode quickly across the yard and broke into a run, leaving the Cushmans behind.

Marc burst through the door, quickly remembering to remove his hat as his ma sat the last bowl on the table.

Will grinned and punched Jack playfully as he said, "Looks like he got here before we ate his share and ours both."

Marc felt the old big brother feelings begin to surface.

"You boys eat my share, and I get to take it out of your hides after dinner."

He playfully poked Jack in the ribs as he settled onto the bench beside him. Their parents shared a smile. They joined hands and bowed their heads to say grace. His father cleared his throat and began.

"Dear Lord, for that which we are about to receive, we are truly grateful. Please bless it to our bodies' nourishment. Lord, thank you for bringing our son home. We know you understand how it feels to have a son come home. Thank you for allowing ours to return. In Jesus' name, amen."

They all shared a smile as their eyes opened from prayer. Jack recovered quickly as his stomach rumbled with the ever-increasing appetite of youth. He reached quickly for the biscuits and placed one in his mouth and one on his plate before passing them to Will. Marc's eyebrows shot up, and he grinned at his ma.

"I bet he's been eating my share the whole time I've been gone."

She returned the smile and nodded. "He sure has

tried. Marc, tell us about Texas. I hear they have only a few trees and a lot of dust."

Marc shook his head. "That's true for some parts of the state, but not all. It really is amazing. The eastern part, where Boyd is from, is green. Lots of trees, farmland. The central part has hills and canyons and a different variety of trees than the eastern area. The western portion is more flat, the way you are saying, yet it also has a beauty that is unique. When you are lying under the stars, and the cattle are soft shadows, calling forlornly to each other, it is so open and free. There are also parts where I haven't been. It is a big state."

His eyes were sparkling with excitement. She saw that it had been a good place for her son and she was glad. His letters had not given many descriptions of the state, just the work he was doing.

"Do you want to go back?" she asked.

All eyes were on him, and he bent his head as he scooped a bite of peas into his mouth. He chewed and swallowed as he decided how to word his response.

"I'm not sure. Mr. Pierce would like Boyd and me to come back and help with the cattle drive to Kansas. John has already decided to settle here. I plan to take a few months to decide. I've been able to save up some, so I don't have to know now."

His father covered his mother's hand with his own and met Marc's eyes.

"Son, take all the time you need. Things are still changing in our state, and it may be more people

34 ~ LANA LYNNE

leaving as well as coming before our state and the nation settle."

"Hey, Marc, can we go see that horse of yours?"

The younger brothers' faces were expectant. Marc grinned as he imagined them trying to ride his mustang back before he was saddle broke. He stood up, and that was all it took. They were out of the door ahead of him. He shook his head at his parents and hurried to catch them before they spooked Ol' Sage.

It was two hours later when they returned to the house and fell into bed. He had answered all their questions about cattlemen, branding, anything he had written about in his letters. His brothers were wonders. He had no doubt that one of them would be able to win young Alice's hand in marriage one day.

∾

He was dreaming of cattle in the expanse of Texas, the star-filled sky that never seemed to end, when suddenly a dust storm rolled in and he couldn't see. The dust then turned to smoke, the sound of a howitzer shell exploding, and the cattle were now men and boys standing shoulder to shoulder as they advanced on the field of battle. Screams of pain surrounded him, and he looked at the men still advancing with him. The screaming continued.

Strong but gentle arms were holding him. He frowned; then a familiar voice soothed him.

"Marcus, it's all right. You're home. Ma's here."

His eyes flew open, and he looked into his mother's face. How many times had he, as well as the other boys in the terrible fray, longed for a mother's comfort. He knew he was grown now, but in that instant it did not matter. In these nightmares that plagued him, he was still the farm boy who was, deep inside, scared of never walking away from the battles. His company had fought so bravely. Tears were now coursing down his face, and he clung to the woman who had brought him into this world.

Emily held her son, stroking the back of his sweat-drenched head and neck. There had been many sleepless nights spent in prayer. As a mother, she wanted to be in all places for him, but she realized at those helpless moments God would be the one who would be able to reach and comfort him. Now she gratefully embraced her son, trying to soothe away the nightmares of battle, so different from the ones that had disrupted his childhood slumber, as the flood of pent-up emotion encompassed them both. They would not speak of this night when morning came. The glimpse into the depths of a youth's painful memories would be ended, and she would not embarrass the man he was now by discussing the torment that had disrupted his sleep. She prayed, in time, the images that swirled in his dreams would lessen and sleep would once again bring rest. Marc's shoulders shuddered as he pulled away and lay back on his pillow. She reached down and smoothed the hair from his forehead, smiling as her hand trailed to the mustache now covering his upper lip.

"You only had peach fuzz when you left," she said, smiling.

He grinned and said, "Oh, Ma," as he gently nudged her hand away from the facial hair now in discussion. "I was thinking of shaving it off. John had a full beard but shaved it before we left Texas. Boyd laughed at him and said it was a good thing he wasn't going back on the cattle trail with a boy's face. You will meet Boyd tomorrow."

"I gather Mr. Richards is more like your father in covering his face with a beard. Well, just tell him to leave John alone. John will find it easier to find a young lady without those scratchy whiskers. It takes a special woman to abide them," she declared, patting the bed soundly.

She and Lee had married so young, it was a few years before he had grown enough facial hair to be considered a beard. It still reddened her face when he kissed her, but she knew she would miss it if he ever removed it.

"I don't think courting will be on Boyd's mind for a long time, Ma." He glanced away and then back at her now puzzled face. "He has lost almost everyone in his life that was dear to him. It is not my place to elaborate until I see he is ready for you to know. He is very private, and John and I have come to respect that. The three of us have helped each other survive."

She reached and took his hand. "Your survival was overseen by one far greater than your friends." She placed a quieting finger to his lips as he started to speak. "I know that your friends were instruments. Son, have you turned away from the walk you started so long ago?"

Marc struggled with finding the right words. "No, Ma, I haven't turned away. It has been a different sort of battle inside. You see and experience so many bad things, it can make you doubt and be disillusioned. To be honest, I was not doing so well on the day we were released. I had prayed and could feel the Lord with me even in the midst of the bloodiest battles; yet in the gloom of that damp prison, the coldness engulfed my very being. I was bitter and very ill. Boyd was the only one walking well when they took us to Virginia and let us go. This past year has taught me many things, but the most important has been that you may hide from people and circumstances for a while, but you can't hide from God. Working cattle is hard, and you go to bed tired. Ma, as I would look up at the stars and the only sounds came from the crickets and cows, I would feel him with me, and then I started praying again. That's the reason John and I came home. John has only recently found his peace. Boyd is still so angry and bitter. He is not willing to talk to anyone, including John or me, about what has happened. He was not raised like we were," he said softly. "Anyway, I am sorry I woke you."

Emily stood, her heart more at peace than it had been, and straightened the bed covers. "I'm not. Goodnight, Son."

She took the candle, which glimmered in the darkness, and left the room.

Chapter

Three

The dew-sparkled grass glistened in the morning light as Florence made her way toward town. Her brother's house was right at the edge of town. Richard had rented it after his marriage. It needed a lot of work. The previous owner, Mr. Bryant, had been killed during the war. His wife and children were unable to maintain it during the war years and had moved to be with relatives.

Jenny, Richard's wife, was expecting their first child very soon. She was having difficulty getting everything done because of the swelling in her ankles. Therefore, Florence had been designated to come by and help out each morning. Pa had excused her from her regular chores, and Florence liked the change.

The town would be more active today as it was Saturday, and the farmers who lived farther out would be coming in for supplies. The ferries were already busy on the Ouachita. The large rocks that lined the banks were in sight. It was so good to feel life proceeding in a more normal fashion. There had

HOME ALWAYS BECKONS ~ 39

been a time when her parents had not allowed their family to go into town. General Steele's troops had built a bridge across the river and had invaded their town. Florence shuddered when she thought of the destruction that had been done by those soldiers. They had been so happy when he moved on to Arkadelphia, yet apprehensive for the people there. Her aunt lived there. However, he kept marching, being given Union reinforcements from Ft. Smith. Word had reached them that Steele had taken Camden, and their hearts had despaired. Her father thought nothing would stop the General at that point. Then a furloughed soldier had passed through and told them Steele had returned to Little Rock after the Union supply wagons had been captured. Without supplies the company in blue was unable to continue their march to Texas.

Florence smiled as she approached the small wooden farmhouse. Her pa had teased her brother when he rented it. He said that it was so close to the river that it should be a ferry. If the river rose, as it had in the past, it could sweep the house away as it had the town's first bridge. She laughed at her father's exaggeration. The house was far enough away from the riverbank as not to be overtaken but close enough that the water could wash the back of the barn. Flooding was serious, but they had learned there were many things that were not under their control. They took it day by day and tried to find reasons to smile.

Richard was repairing the woodshed beside the

house as Florence made her way across the yard. He paused, board in hand, at her approach.

"Good morning, sunshine." He smiled as she reached him. "Jenny will be so glad you're here."

She pretended to pout. "And you're not? I am so hurt … my own brother."

In one quick movement, Richard laid the board down and advanced toward her.

She moved quickly, as sisters do when brothers are after them, running toward the house, calling, "Jenny, save me!" then dissolving in laughter as her brother caught her and swept her into a big hug, followed by a well-deserved tickling.

Her sister-in-law opened the door and, with mock sternness, addressed her husband.

"Richard, will you please let her go. She will be of no use to me if you tickle all the air out of her," she said.

Jenny smiled as her husband obliged her by releasing his sister. He came over to his wife, kissed her forehead, glared playfully at his sister, and returned to his work. Florence smiled in a companionable way and followed her sister-in-law inside.

"Florey, I am so glad you are here. My ankles are so swollen that I couldn't put on my shoes," Jenny said, raising her dress slightly to reveal her enlarged bare feet. "It looks like you will have to do all the cooking for today, as well as tomorrow."

Florence watched her move to the wooden rocker and sink down heavily. Tendrils from her restrained, raven-black hair clung to her damp forehead, and she dabbed at it absently with the back of her hand.

Jenny glanced up at her and said, "I'm sorry to be so useless."

"You don't have to apologize. The work you will soon face with my new niece or nephew should more than make up for any work you can't do now. Please just sit there and talk to me as I work. It will go by faster that way. I get tired working without anyone to talk to. Besides, I've got news." Florence paused in gathering the utensils needed to begin the meal preparations for the day and looked directly into Jenny's dark eyes. "John and Marc came home yesterday."

Jenny maintained her gaze momentarily and then nodded toward the window. "When are you going to tell Richard?" she asked with her voice full of aching for the pain and anger that could wash forth when the three men would come face to face.

Richard had been Jenny's rescuer many times in her life. As a young girl of ten, when her family had moved to Rockport, he had stood up for her when some of the other children had not wanted the "squaw girl" to play. The fourteen-year-old boy had walked boldly into the middle of the taunting crowd, challenging anyone to argue with his comments, which soundly shamed and dispersed the group, and then turned to ask Jenny if she was going to be all right. Florence had known as Richard had left the schoolyard with Dawn, Alice, and her that day that he would forever be a part of Jenny's life. The years and events that followed had born out that

42 ~ LANA LYNNE

knowledge. Now she knew Jenny thought it was time to try and protect him. Jenny looked expectantly at Florence.

"I'm not sure we should tell him. You see, Ma has asked their families to church and lunch tomorrow. He will find out in a group, and then the three, or should I say four, of them will have to be nice to each other. Don't you think?" Florence reasoned.

Jenny shook her head as she struggled to her feet and walked to the window.

"No, I don't. Richard would feel betrayed if we don't prepare him. And what do you mean by 'four'? Who is with John and Marc?"

"A man named Boyd Richards. I'm sure Richard has spoken of him. He was in the Texas brigade of the army of Northern Virginia that their regiment joined with in late 1862. I haven't met him, nor have I seen John; only Marc. He and his pa came over yesterday to fetch Will and Jack. Jen, he has been through a lot too."

Florence backed up a step as Jenny turned to face her, eyes blazing.

Jenny advanced quicker than Florence had seen her move in a month as she shouted, "What about everyone else? That's the whole problem. No one here has ever questioned that any of our boys and men had been through unspeakable experiences. Talk to our neighbors who are in the Invalid Corps in Arkadelphia. But they would have gladly come home to help their families rebuild if they could have. Marc and John could have, and they didn't. Don't you see the difference?"

Two days ago, a part of her would have agreed with Jen, but after seeing Marc she wasn't sure. There had been something in his eyes. She and Dawn had spoken about it as they were going to sleep last night. Even Dawn, who had been so hurt when Marc had not returned, was letting go of those feelings. Florence was just about to answer Jen when the sound of angry voices reached them. They exchanged knowing looks and rushed to the door.

They flung open the door in time to see Richard knock Marcus to the ground. Marcus shook his head and then sprung up and was about to return the blow when John and Boyd flanked him with restraining arms. Jenny moved between the two men and laid gentle hands on Richard's tense arms. She glanced up at the angry faces that were surrounding her.

"No, Richard. Not this way," she pleaded.

Richard kept his stormy gaze on Marc. "Jen, go back in the house. It is past time for this to be settled. It may never be settled." He caught the movement of his sister moving toward them and turned his head. "Florey, you knew they were here. Why didn't you tell me?" And then, as she started to answer, he held up his hand. "No, don't. I probably know why. Just take Jen to the house for me, please." He held his younger sister's imploring stare and shook his head. "Now!"

When he was sure the ladies were back inside, he turned to face his three former comrades in arms.

Richard's gray eyes narrowed as he saw Marc's jaw muscles clenching in anger.

"I guess it's time you explained your cowardly behavior," he said sarcastically. "All of you." He steadily met the three pairs of eyes that were focused on him.

Marc looked too angry to speak. John squeezed Marc's arm before releasing it, nodded to Boyd to confirm that he would keep Marc restrained, and then stepped directly in front of Richard. He had an inch in height above the slightly younger man and was glad to have the advantage as he spoke.

"Richard, there are a lot of things you don't understand, and even if we list them all, it may not make sense. But there were a lot of senseless events during these past years. We are not going to make them go away or change them. All we can do is to try to get past them. First, I want to thank you for being with Matt at the end. Ma told me last night. It should have been me there. Maybe I could have protected him ... I don't know."

He paused as emotion threatened to overtake him. Flashes of memories of the last battle in which he had fought besieged him. The face of his little brother amidst the cannon smoke at Gettysburg as they advanced shoulder to shoulder, then the sensation of feeling himself fall as he had felt the fire in his side.

Matt had been engaged in hand-to-hand fighting beside him at the time, but as soon as his adversary had fallen, he had rushed to John's side. They had been motioned to fall back, but Matt wouldn't leave him. Richard, Marc, and Boyd had reached them at this point and finally convinced Matt to fall back with Richard, leaving Marc and Boyd to move John to safety. Richard and Matt had made it to safety, but Marc and Boyd were captured, along with John as they were trying to pull him behind some trees. That was the last time he had seen Matt.

John looked down into Richard's face.

"Although, it was you who got him to safety the last time I saw him."

Richard could see the memories overtaking John. He remembered the promise he had made to Matt at Chickamauga. He could see the pain-filled eyes of the fifteen-year-old as he gripped his hand in the dressing station. The blood had been pouring from the stomach wound, which Matt was clutching with one hand as he clung to Richard with the other. Carl Wilkins had also suffered a wound, although less serious, and was unable to be there. Matt had been passed over by the surgeon in favor of a less severely wounded soldier. Richard had known then that the wound was mortal. Matt's breath had been ragged as he extracted his friend's vow.

"Richard, promise me ... if you and John make it home ... no matter what ... you will be his brother for me. He will help you. I know."

Richard had been willing and had wanted that so much, but John had never come home. Not even when he could have. He did not want to hold onto

46 ~ LANA LYNNE

that with John, for Matt's sake, but he wasn't ready to give John complete absolution just yet.

"John, I promised Matt that I would be your brother since he could not remain. It was his wish for us to help each other, but you didn't come home."

Richard saw the tears fill John's serious eyes. He saw Marc and Boyd swallow hard before turning away to give them a moment, and for an instant he almost felt their old friendship. Then he shook his head and focused on John.

John reached out his hand, but Richard wouldn't take it. He stiffened as the normally reserved John pulled him into an embrace that mourned Matt and all the losses of war. Richard kept his arms to his sides and pulled away after a moment. He was bound by a promise to forgive John at some point, even if he wasn't ready at this moment, but not Marc and Boyd. Marc had been his best friend, and Boyd … that was a puzzle and a disappointment. He stepped around John and crossed to the blonde-haired man beside the woodshed.

"Explain something to me, Boyd. Why didn't you send these boys home, and why didn't you go home? You, who was always talking about his precious, what was her name? Oh, yeah. Nancy. And weren't you supposed to have a child?"

"Richard, don't."

Marc placed a restraining hand on Richard's arm as he stepped closer to the man who had visibly turned to granite as Richard's words whipped at him. Richard glared at Marc and jerked his arm away, continuing his advance.

Richard did not heed the signs John and Marc had come to read and respect. Boyd's stony stare never wavered from Richard as he appraised the approaching enemy. One hand began to slowly stroke his bearded face. Richard continued as he reached the rigid figure.

"Did you just skip over your homecoming like these two and run away to be with the cows? What? I don't hear an answer."

It happened so fast no one could have stopped him. Boyd grabbed Richard by the throat and pinned him against the wall of the woodshed. His voice was low and clipped.

"I think it is time for you to be quiet and listen. When I finish, you will not question Marc about anything he doesn't want to talk about. Hopefully, you will realize how stupid it is to throw away his friendship."

Marcus and John were momentarily frozen with shock. They had known that all the pent up bitterness and anger would erupt in Boyd one day. Their friend had turned very taciturn after the war; the epitome of a silent, ever simmering fire waiting to erupt. Boyd seemed to notice Florence and Jenny, who had reemerged as they saw the scene from the window, and loosened his grip around Richard's throat a little before continuing. The closely guarded floodgate had opened and no one could stop it.

"I notice your wife is expecting. How nice for

you. And, yes, my Nancy was expecting as I left for war. My younger brother was staying with her and was to take care of them while I was away. We didn't think the war would last as long as it did. My one comfort was that Ben was with them. When I no longer got letters when I was in prison, I thought they just couldn't get through. Marc and John almost died in prison and could not travel alone when we were released. I thought I would take them home and let Nancy help me get them better." Marcus stepped forward and laid a gentle hand on his friend's shoulder, which was easily and angrily shrugged off. Boyd turned briefly, his golden eyes blazing before returning his attention to Richard. Marc knew he had to let the tragic tale be told and stepped back beside John. They would intervene if he endangered Richard. Boyd's words continued, "So it took us awhile to get back to Texas. It was obvious as we traveled that things had changed everywhere, but I was still anticipating stepping on my land and holding my family. I breathed a sigh of relief when I saw the house was still there and smoke was coming from the chimney. I pulled up the wagon in front of the cabin, expecting the door to open and Nancy to come out with our son—she had written me after his birth. But the door did not open quickly. Instead, after a moment, I heard a thumping on the wood floor before the door opened to reveal my younger brother, now with a cane to lean on, and minus a leg. After the shock of the fact that Ben had fought in the war registered, I asked for Nancy. Ben hung his head before he told me that Nancy and Sam, my son, were dead. I called him a liar. I ran into the yard and called for her, and then I saw the two crosses under the pecan tree. Ben explained that during the last year of the war a group of our graycoats had come by, starving, demanding food. You know how mean men can get when they are hungry; it doesn't matter what side you're on. They did not have much, but Nancy had fed them. Then they threatened them if Ben didn't leave with them. New fighting boys were hard to find at that point. He had to go or Nancy and Sam would have been harmed by our own soldiers. Ben had gotten home a month before we arrived and found … ," Boyd paused his staccato narrative at this point and looked down briefly before once again locking his gaze with a very pale Richard's, "a poorly dug small grave under the tree and Nancy on the bed inside. She had been dead a couple of days. We did not have any close neighbors, so I don't know what happened for sure, but Ben did find out that there had been some people in the nearest community who had died of a fever about that time. She was alone with our child as he died, buried him alone, and then died alone. I wasn't there to protect them or to take care of them. Now, I know you found devastation here, but did you find that? No! Marc and John were recovering and struggling, but no matter what they say, I know that in the end the decision to go to South Texas and work cattle was more for me than them. I couldn't stay on my farm; too many memories. Ben had met a boy from the next county on his way home; they had walked

50 ~ LANA LYNNE

and talked, as did many returning soldiers. He came from a large family, and Ben was going to try to get him to come help him with the farm until I could come back and face it. I still can't."

The hand around Richard's throat dropped. Boyd's golden eyes slowly focused on the tearful faces of Jenny and Florence. He stepped back from Richard, who was watching him in stunned silence and rubbing his throat.

"Ma'am, I didn't mean any disrespect to your delicate condition," he said and then turned to Richard. "Whatever you faced when you got home, you had family to face it with you. Don't begrudge me the help of these friends. Outside of Ben, they are all I've got."

Marc wiped a hand wearily over his face and glanced sideways at John, both exchanging looks of quiet disbelief at the extent of their friend's narrative. Time and friendship had done little to comfort Boyd; he needed help that far exceeded earthly solutions. John started forward as Boyd turned.

"Don't, John. Just leave it be," said Boyd. He nodded to Marc as he left. It had been a long time since he had even spoken of Nancy. Now he needed to be alone for a while. The solitary walk back to Wilkins' farm would help.

There was deafening silence following Boyd's departure. Then Jenny moved to Richard. He assured her that he was all right and needed to finish his work. John stepped in and picked up the board Richard had been about to nail to the woodshed. He shoved

Richard, who was now coughing slightly, toward the house. Richard went with an arm around Jenny but turned before they reached the door.

"Marc, I'd like to talk later," he said.

Marcus met his eyes and nodded, suddenly overcome with weariness. He felt so old and tired. He heard the hammer hit the nail as John began to work. That's what he needed: work, something to engage him mentally and physically. As he started to pick up another board to help John with the job, he realized that Florence had not moved and was staring at him.

"I'm sorry you had to hear all of that," he said, watching as her gray eyes shifted upward to his chin.

He lifted a hand to touch it and found that blood was trickling downward from his upper lip.

Florence impulsively grabbed his hand and led him beside the riverbank. She gently prodded him to sit on a large rock before she tore a piece of her petticoat, dipped it in the water, and returned to him. He grimaced slightly as she wiped it a little roughly.

"Sorry," she apologized and dabbed it more gently. "It's hard to get out of your mustache. There, all done." She stepped back. "I better go help Jenny."

Suddenly, as she headed to the house, things felt a little awkward. Marc did not want that. The morning had been filled with so many painful memories. It was time to find something pleasant to share.

"Tadpole!" he called and grinned, a little painfully, as she turned and frowned at him.

"Marcus Johnson, no one has called me that for—"

"Over five years," he finished for her. "Well, I'm back now, and I need my old fishing charm. The boys and I never caught as many fish if you didn't tag along. You want to go fishing?"

Florence felt like a little girl again, but she wouldn't admit it.

"I had stopped fishing with you a good year before you left; an insufferable lot, all of you."

Marc had always wondered about that. Now he noticed that she had side-stepped his question.

"So, do you want to get John, hopefully Richard, maybe Boyd, and go fishing before supper?" he asked with an encouraging grin.

He saw the young woman hesitate and then the little girl, who was not too far below the surface, win.

She smiled impishly and answered, "Yes, if I get all my work done, and if you can convince Dawn to go."

Her smile broadened at his groan.

"Florence, Dawn never liked fishing. The one time I got her to go, right before I left, she complained the whole time. I'll take her on a picnic another day." He saw her stubborn look. "Fine, I'll do it."

"Good. Now, I better get to cooking if there is to be enough food for today's and tomorrow's meals," she said with satisfaction.

"Florence, convince Richard to come. I'm going to help John for a bit and then go find Boyd. I also need to help Pa finish repairs on the barn. We will bring Will, Jack, Alice, and Dawn when we meet. Bring John and Richard to our old fishing spot on the river about three o'clock."

Marcus pulled out his pocket-watch. It was now seven o'clock in the morning, and that should give enough time.

She nodded and went into the house. He made his way to the woodshed and began working beside John. They worked in silence, the way they often did, until the job was finished. The last board had been nailed when they saw Richard emerge from the house. Marc held his breath.

A warm wind blew dust up across the yard as Richard made his way toward them. Marc shifted uncomfortably as the red-haired man reached him. He adjusted his hat slightly lower on his forehead so his eyes could not be clearly seen. It was a habit he had acquired to make sure he had a chance to read another man's face first. However, as his old friend stopped in front of him, he could see that the shutters were firmly in place. Neither one was going to let this be easy, even after the morning's events.

Come on, Richard, Marc thought. *Let's bridge this gap.*

Wait a minute! Why was he waiting on Richard to do it? These thoughts propelled him forward. He took one finger and shoved back his hat a bit, revealing guarded eyes.

"So, are we going fishing?" he asked.

Across Richard's face passed looks of bewilderment, irritation, and finally humor.

"Tarnation, Marc. It was a lot easier to be mad at you when you weren't here."

"You did a pretty good job earlier," Marc countered as he gingerly touched his cut lip.

Richard frowned at him. "That's nothing. You're lucky the ladies rescued you."

"You're lucky Boyd remembered that he liked you."

"About that…" Richard looked remorseful. "I had no right to question him. Believe me, the pain I feel for him at this moment won't be forgotten; especially now that I have Jenny. It had somehow gotten into my mind that he had deserted Nancy."

"In all the gore that the war showed me, the one that chilled me the most was the sight of Boyd after Ben told him. The scream of pain as he fell on her grave still haunts me," John gruffly interjected.

John clenched his eyes shut at the memory, shuddering with the depth of the other man's pain. Upon opening them, he found the other men quietly sharing his feelings; one with firsthand knowledge.

"Richard, we couldn't let him destroy himself after we had helped each other survive for so long. I don't regret that. I do regret being gone so long. John and I could have left after a few months. It just became easier not to. The pain we had seen in war, in prison, with Boyd's loss, and whatever y'all may have been facing here, became less real the longer we stayed. In that respect, we were wrong. You've

HOME ALWAYS BECKONS ~ 55

never let me down. I'm sorry you faced coming home alone," said Marc.

There was a pause as Richard made a decision.

"Boys, come with me. It's time you took a walk through town."

He made sure he saw tentative agreement in their eyes before turning and purposefully heading toward the very nearby road that ran through town.

The trio strode past the courthouse, which was in the process of construction. How well they all remembered that twenty-fourth day of June 1861 in front of that building when their company had been presented with a flag as they left for Little Rock. They saw the doctor's house, the church/school, the post office, the general stores, the saloons, the blacksmith's shop, the lawyer's house, and finally wove their way to the tannery shop by the river. Familiar faces were spotted as hands waved and old friends called out to them as they made their way, but Richard was not willing to stop, so they politely waved and promised to visit later. Now Richard stopped and pointed to the doorway of a small structure.

"I'm not sure if you remember Doc's little boy. Well, he was five years old when Steele's men came through and was here watching things. One of those soldiers shot him." He paused and then started walking, pointing out things as he went. "There's the old house of that 'Arkansas Drum Maker' and fiddle player. Even though he fought with us, I keep remembering that he made drums for the Yanks as well as us. Those drums kept going—to the death."

They continued their walk to the mill and various other local sights. Richard gave the narrative of the devastation Steele's troops had dealt the farms and plantations in their county. The plight of the slaves during the war was terrible, and now dealing with their new freedom after it was daunting, but welcome, for most of them. Only a few of their relatives had ever had slaves, and it had never been an issue without contention. Their walk finally took them to a deserted cabin, which all recognized as Jenny's old home.

Richard opened the door to floating dust and darkness. He advanced and stood in the shadows for a moment before speaking. His voice was roughened by emotion.

"You may not have realized it, but I knew that Jenny was the one for me since the first day I saw her in the schoolyard. I downplayed it. Then her mother died that year before the war. Jenny was so vulnerable and sad. Pa would come over to help her father. Not many would be around him because he was married to an Indian. The ladies in town were so harsh when her ma died, like it was a sign that their marriage was wrong. Our mothers had been the only ones to be kind to her. Well, the war came and her pa would not leave Jenny until Pa came home wounded. He felt he must do his part. Jenny was to stay with my family, but she kept coming up here to check on things. Anyway, one day some of the guerrillas who

HOME ALWAYS BECKONS ~ 57

were passing through came by while she was here. They raided what was left in the smokehouse and then entered the house. Jenny had hidden in a trunk, but they found her."

A wave of anger coursed through him, and his hands clenched and unclenched several times before he continued.

"She ran out into the yard and fought back, and they hit her several times. However, she remembered some of the things her mother had taught her. She collapsed, as if dead, and held her breath. I'm not sure this would have stopped them long, but it caused them to pause long enough that they were not prepared for a group of our returning men; believe it or not, one of them was me. There were only three of them and a handful of us, but it was enough. As soon as they scattered, I rushed to her side, and she fought like a wildcat again until she recognized me. She began crying hysterically, and I scooped her up to take her home. She was nothing but skin and bones. Our group became grimmer as we saw more of our families. There had been so much devastation."

Richard turned to them. "That's when I wished for you two. The war had been lost, but I would not concede my friends, my family, and my town. The boys that came home all had the same determination. Each day I worked, I would look toward the road, thinking you'd be there."

Marc and John were both silent. What could they say? Their place should have been here. How could they justify anything, even given Boyd's need?

58 ~ LANA LYNNE

Marc ran a hand through his hair. It was time to stop this.

"Richard, I'm sorry. That is all I can say. I know it does not change a thing or the consequences. In time, I want to rebuild our friendship. But can we, at this point, move forward? We are all weary of the events that have brought us here, and we will never forget; yet it is time to find the good that is left. You and Jenny are about to be parents. A new life will start who knows nothing of this pain," he implored.

John moved to Richard and placed a hand on his shoulder.

"Quit carrying the whole world on your shoulders, and let God handle it. It's the only way I was able to come home."

Richard stared at John for a long moment before hanging his head and nodding. It was time to forgive. A grin suddenly broke out on his face.

Marc saw it and began smiling himself. "What's the joke?" he asked.

The grin broadened. "Did you really promise Florey you'd make Dawn come fishing?"

"Yeah!"

"I wouldn't miss this for anything." Richard headed out the door.

John and Marc were quick to follow. The old feelings of camaraderie flowed as they moved toward the town. Richard suddenly stopped in front of the general store, filled with brotherly mischief. His two companions glimpsed the look on his face and shared equally mischievous grins, eyes sparkling.

"Do you remember the last time Dawn went with us? She was what? Ten, eleven?" Richard saw them nod in agreement before he continued. "She screamed every time a bug landed or flew near her. Marc, she ran and hid behind you every time until you put that lizard on her bonnet. Then she ran home screaming she would never trust any of us again."

The group all laughed at the memory.

"And remember, she was trying to be so lady-like as she left with her nose in the air—until she tripped on her dress hem as she scrambled up the hill," John added, his eyes watering in mirth at the recollection.

Richard smirked. "Fellas, she's still scared of bugs, fish on a line, or anything of the like. Shall we have some fun?"

"Definitely," agreed John.

"Oh, yeah," said Marc.

"That's settled. Now, we better get back. I know you both have work to do at your folks'. I'll finish up at home and get Jenny and Florey to put some food in a basket for dinner. We might as well eat by the river. You two can pick up Dawn and meet us."

Their truce was fragile, but they all walked with lighter hearts and steps as they headed back to work.

John had barely been able to convince Boyd to join them at the river. It had taken extra persuasion from Mrs. Wilkins. John could tell Boyd had a soft spot for her. Boyd barely remembered his own mother. His uncle had raised him and his brother until he had left home at fifteen. He had been unwilling to help his uncle with the business end of running their Georgia plantation. He could not agree with slavery. Nancy had lived on a neighboring farm, and he had convinced her folks to allow them to be married. He had money that had been left for him and his brother by his parents. They had been able to go to Texas and start their farm with it.

John and Boyd arrived just after Florence, Richard, and Jenny. Jenny had already found a rock on which to prop her feet. Richard was putting string on their poles, and Florence was hunting for bait. Richard caught Boyd's look of apprehension and motioned him over with a grin.

"I think you better give me a hand before the rest get here, especially my sister. We won't be able to concentrate once she arrives," he said.

Boyd sighed in relief and looked questioningly at Florence. "I take it is your other sister, Dawn, to whom you refer?"

Florence interrupted them. "Oh, he's just being mean. Dawn does not like to fish at all. The worms, the wiggling fish, the dragonflies, or anything like that. But she is great with sewing, cooking, or tending animals."

She playfully pushed her brother as she walked past with the bucket of bait and placed it on the ground beside the poles.

"He and the boys tricked her awful the last time she came. She hasn't come back since."

She turned to see her brother's guilty face. "No, no, no! Jenny, please influence your husband to behave." She inclined her head toward her sister-in-law.

Jenny was already shaking her head. "That, I'm afraid, is not in our control. You will have to guard her. I won't be any help in my present condition."

Richard turned to Florence with a smug look. "So there, little sister."

Just then, the sound of horses stole their attention. Marc and Dawn had obviously been racing on their way. Dawn's cheeks were flushed, and a few tendrils of golden hair were blowing around her face from under her bonnet. Her blue eyes danced. Florence was a little surprised. It usually took a lot to convince Dawn to race and never anyone else but her sisters. That is, except Marc one time before, long ago. Evidently Alice and the boys weren't coming.

It was then that Florence noticed Boyd almost gaping at her sister. *Well, well, what was that about?* That man was too complicated for her to even begin to think about. It hurt her heart and her head to think about what she had heard this morning. She was good at watching people. She found their actions usually demonstrated more of who they were than their words.

She quickly crossed to Dawn, who had dismounted and was tethering her horse to a low tree branch. Once Marc had made sure she didn't need help, he had crossed to where the other men stood.

62 ~ LANA LYNNE

Florence glanced over her shoulder at them as she reached her sister.

"How did Marc convince you to join us? I thought you said you would never go fishing again?" Florence asked.

Dawn's eyes twinkled. "Marc was hard to refuse when he asked so nicely."

"I thought you learned what a prankster he was years ago. Don't kid yourself; they will tease you to no end today."

"Oh, Florey, they've grown up. It will be fine." She saw Jenny wave. "I'm going to check on Jen. Did you get all the chores done at their place?"

"Yes, dear sister," Florence said as she followed Dawn to sit beside Jenny on the large rock.

After they sat, the male group moved toward them, looking not so much like the men they had become as they boys they had been.

Richard coughed slightly as he tried to sound serious. "Ladies, you are looking nice this afternoon. Is your pleasure to watch us catch your meal or to help us in our task?"

Dawn looked slightly uncomfortable but firmly said, "We will help, of course. That is, Florence and me. Jenny will need to stay right here, don't you think, Richard?"

Richard winked at his wife as he said, "Of course." He then nodded at Florence and Dawn. "Shall we?"

Florence and Dawn shared a glance that said, *Our brother is never this polite to us.* Something was definitely planned. Still, they made their way to the water's edge, and Florence reached for two poles. John quickly reached her and removed the poles.

"No, those are the longer ones. Try these; they should be better."

Florence began inspecting the poles but could not find anything overtly wrong, so she shrugged and handed one to Dawn. She then reached for the bait bucket.

Dawn peered cautiously over the rim at the wriggling worms. *I can do this!* she told herself, swallowing hard. She gingerly reached a hand inside and then quickly jerked back as her hand felt the wiggly, cold skin. A shudder passed through her as she closed her eyes tightly. She heard barely suppressed snickers and glared at her brother and his friends. After pulling herself up proudly, she boldly reached in and came out with a worm between her right thumb and forefinger. She glared triumphantly at the group and then back uncertainly at the worm.

"Now, what do I do with you?"

Thank goodness for her younger sister. Florence quickly took the worm from her unresisting fingers and threaded him on the hook. Dawn followed her to a grassy patch and sat down. Florence quickly threw her line out and Dawn followed suit. That wasn't so bad. It did not matter that she was now a little mad at Marcus for not rescuing her. Her sister was right. She knew there had been a reason her feelings had changed before he left. She was beginning to remember why. The foursome—John, Marc, Richard, and Matt—had been full of mischief given the

64 ~ LANA LYNNE

chance. Their parents had made them spend days and sometimes weeks apart due to their escapades. Matt had loved to imitate the older boys. He was gone now. She glanced at Florence, Matt had secretly been stuck on her, and Dawn had thought... Well, a lot was not as they had thought. Anyway, it seemed they now had another fourth participant in their games. Boyd's burnished head was bent as he placed his bait on the hook. His skin was tanned golden brown, and she could see he had well-muscled arms as he threw the fishing line. Suddenly, he turned his head, and she encountered the most amazing eyes she had ever seen. They looked like the eyes of the mountain lion she had seen when she visited her cousins in the Ozark Mountains when she was younger. She felt her face grow warm and quickly looked toward the river. A glance at Florence assured her that her sister was deep in thought and had not observed her flustered reaction.

"How long does it take to catch a fish?" she asked Florence.

"The more you talk, the longer it takes," Florence responded pointedly.

"Oh."

There was silence for about a fifteen-minute period. Then Dawn felt a jerk on her line. Florence also saw it and put down hers. She knew her older sister would require help removing the fish if she caught it.

Dawn was beginning to get excited and stood up with her pole in hand. The fish was a nice size and popped out of the water one time. Dawn jerked hard in one direction as he pulled hard in the other. Suddenly it was over. The line slid off the pole and the fish swam away.

The sisters stood there in disbelief. What had happened? The line had not broken. Florence quickly picked up her pole for a second inspection. This time she saw it. A slip knot! They had been sabotaged! She whirled on the culprits who were now laughing openly.

"You did this? It's not funny. She almost caught her first fish. You should be ashamed," she fumed.

The men just stood, sat, and rolled there in laughter. The deeper Florence frowned and stood there with her hands on her hips, the harder they laughed; all that is except for Mr. Richards. He did have an almost suppressed grin on his face, but at least he wasn't guffawing like the others. She decided that he was their most dignified escape.

"Mr. Richards, you are the only one quiet enough or sane enough to hear me at this point. We ladies," she paused long enough to get nods from Dawn and Jenny, "would like to go home. Would you be so kind as to be our escort? It seems we can't even count on our brother at this point."

"Ah, Florey, you always liked a good joke. We were just funning. Please stay. We haven't even eaten," Richard implored.

"Whose fault is that? We would have one big fish ready and clean right now. Besides that, Dawn might have started to like fishing if you hadn't been so childish."

Florence glanced at her sister, who, to her dismay, was now trying to hide a smile. Well, that was it! Why was she trying to defend someone who now appeared to be enjoying the situation? She threw up her hands in exasperation and asked, "Not you, too? Fine then, you stay here and let them laugh at your expense." She turned to Jenny to inquire, "Jen?"

Jenny struggled to her feet. "Richard, I think I better go home and lie down. My ankles are so sore, and if you make me laugh anymore I'm libel to go into labor right here."

Richard crossed to help her. "I'll take you," he said.

Jen waved him off as she said, "No, it's good to see you enjoying your friends. Bring home what fish you don't eat." She turned to Boyd. "Mr. Richards, will you be so kind?"

Boyd received a nod from Richard. He expelled a breath and stepped forward as he responded, "Certainly, ma'am. Ladies, are you ready?"

He moved forward to Jenny. "May I?" he asked then took her elbow as she nodded.

Dawn turned to the remaining threesome. "I have decided the joke at my expense was worth it to see you together again. Good day." She received wide smiles and appreciation from them and a betrayed look from her sister. "Are you coming, Florey?"

Florence could not understand how it had all gotten turned around. She had not played the joke,

HOME ALWAYS BECKONS ~ 67

yet she was the only one who was upset. Secretly she was also glad to see them playing pranks together again, but she couldn't say that now. The reason she had been so mad was that she hoped to help her sister with Marcus. That's why she had insisted on bringing Dawn. Oh, what difference did it make? Now, she had to go back and be inside the rest of the day. She detested the idea. It was her fault, though. "Yeah, you go ahead. I want to walk a little behind."

∾

Marcus had had enough. Florence was acting strangely. He wanted the girl he used to know. She had rescued her sister but still laughed in the past. He strode past Richard and John. Boyd had started out with the ladies, and Florence had taken her first step to go when Marc reached her. Before anyone could guess his intent, he scooped her up and quickly strode to the river and dumped her in the water. She came up sputtering.

"You cool off! Stay there till you've found out it's all right to laugh. You want to, and you know it," Marc said.

Richard and John gaped in disbelief. They did not laugh until they could gage Florence's reaction. They watched as Marc stood there with feet spread and arms crossed in a commanding stance, waiting for her reaction. Seconds seemed like an eternity, the sounds of birds and the water amplified. Then the girlish smile flashed, followed by contagious, self-deprecating laughter.

Boyd and the ladies had turned at the sound of the splash. The sound of relieved laughter spread like wildfire. Marcus stepped forward as Florence struggled out of the water. He was smiling broadly as she placed her hand in his.

He looked at her now sparkling gray eyes and darkened amber hair.

"It seems I keep seeing you in a rather dampened state. Yesterday the rain, and today the river," he said in a good-natured manner.

"I do believe you've cooled me off and drenched me a lot more than the rain. I certainly dampened the day," Florence stated ruefully as she glanced downward and tried to lift the heavy, wet dress away from her.

Marc followed her gaze downward to her clinging dress and felt his face redden. He saw her puzzled look at his obvious discomfort.

"Marc? Are you—," she started.

Just then an all too familiar male voice called to her.

"Florence, what's the meaning of this? Why did you not tell me of this trip? And what are you doing wet? This is not proper. Richard, do you have a blanket?"

Arnold Beasley arrived in an indignant huff. Without waiting for an answer, he crossed to where the abandoned picnic basket sat with a blanket folded on top of it. He quickly unfolded it and crossed to Florence.

Richard reached them and took the blanket from his hands and then securely wrapped his sister in it.

"What's not proper is for you to approach my sister in such a familiar manner. I do not believe you have spoken to my pa about courting her. She does not have to make you aware of all her activities. As her older brother, I am quite capable of seeing after her," Richard said as he protectively wrapped her in the blanket. He then walked her to Dawn and Jenny. "Boyd, please escort the ladies home in the wagon, and we will follow shortly. The day has suddenly lost its appeal."

Arnold's face matched his hair color in embarrassment at being put in his place so publicly.

"I will certainly be speaking to your father this day," he said and then endeavored to leave with as much pride as possible.

John and Marc gathered the fishing gear as Richard and Boyd settled the ladies in the wagon. The sound of wagon wheels signaled their departure.

Richard crossed to the horses and untethered them. "Ready?"

They mounted and began to ride back in silence. Marc did not like the mixed feelings that were suddenly present within him. Florence was Florence—Florey, his little shadow.

"Hey, Richard, your pa's not going to let Arnold court and marry Florence, is he?" Marc asked.

There was a frown between Richard's eyes, which were so like his sister's.

"I don't know. Marc, it's past time for Dawn

and Florence to be courting. You may not have noticed, but Florey is full-grown. The choices aren't that numerous. Even with the stagecoaches coming through town and the river trade bringing in new people. They don't want her to link up with some Yankee passing through or worse. It's better if it's someone they know."

"What about her choices and feelings?"

"Everyone doesn't start out as lucky as Jen and me. I have loved her since before the war. I just couldn't say anything because we had to leave. As much as it galls me, Arnold will be here, and he is steady. A few days ago, I wouldn't have said this, but if either one of you decides to stay around ... No, that's crazy. Isn't it?" Richard encompassed his friends with a probing gaze.

John shook his head. "No, I'm real fond of Florey, Richard, but ... well, Matt was always about Florey, kinda the way you were about Jen, but he was too shy to let on to her. I had it in my mind to be more her brother. You understand?"

There was silence. Richard swallowed hard then asked, "Marc, you were always fond of Dawn. Are you still?"

Marc contemplated his answer before he spoke. "Yes, but not as I was before. I'm not sure we are of that mind. Besides, I'm not sure what I'm going to do. I may have a few more adventures in my future."

They rode in silence the rest of the way to Richard's house. Marc wasn't sure about a lot of things, but he was sure about one thing. Florence was not going to marry Arnold Beasley.

Chapter

Four

She had to court Arnold! Her pa had proudly announced he had agreed to allow Arnold to court her after she and Dawn had come home that evening.

The day had turned out well after Richard got home. Marc and John had decided to go to their own homes, so Boyd also left. Then Richard and Jen convinced Dawn and Florence to stay to supper. They weren't expected home before then anyway.

It was more relaxed than it had been in a long time. Richard seemed to be more jovial and less bitter now that he had made peace with Marc, John, and Boyd. They talked about their childhoods and the happy memories they shared. Siblings completing each other's recollections and feeling more completed by having each other.

Then Richard had taken them home. Pa had been on the porch. He looked satisfied with himself as he made the announcement as they mounted the porch steps. Dawn quickly cast a look of concern toward her sister. Richard looked ill. Florence looked stunned. All the blood drained from her face.

All she could mange was a whispered, "Yes, Pa." and, "May I go to bed now?"

She received a nod and then walked past her ma as if in a daze on her way to the room she shared with her sisters, where she sat on her bed for the longest time.

All this time Arnold had been there; like a fly you could shoo away if it irritated you too long. Now she had to allow him to be around her and had to be cordial. Her pa had given his word. It would not be honorable if he went back on his word. She could not ask him to do that.

Richard saw his mother's concerned face as she came out onto the porch.

"What happened? Was she not pleased?" she asked.

Richard looked at his father's now grim face.

Alan stroked his dimpled chin thoughtfully and frowned.

"No, Ella. She did not appear to be." He glanced at his son and eldest daughter. "Nor do our eldest children seem to be any more pleased than she. Richard?"

"Pa, he tries to command her every action," Richard responded.

"Is that not good? Your sister is very spirited. It will take someone strong to help her take her place as a wife. She has always been our most difficult child. She would run off fishing with you and your friends when she should have been helping her ma. During the war, it was hard to protect her. She wanted to run all over the place. The incident with Jenny is the only thing that finally got through to her."

"Pa, could it not be someone other than Arnold? Surely, there is time to consider others," Dawn tentatively interjected.

The frown turned to a look of exasperation.

"Dawn, the war has delayed the normal course of things. It is time both your sister and you were married. I will not consider any of the new people passing through or newly settled. There is too much uncertainty. I will have my daughters married into good, local families. Arnold has waited as well. He knew Matt was the choice. He waited the appropriate amount of time since the war ended. They are of a good age for marriage." He crossed his arms and fixed her with a probing stare. "Now, daughter, since we are so openly discussing this delicate topic. Should I expect Marcus Johnson to speak with me soon?"

Dawn blushed furiously and her mother smiled at her fondly. Ella crossed to her and put an encouraging arm around her.

"Pa, Marc has only been home a day."

"It appears you enjoyed the outing today. It is long enough to know if there is a semblance of the feelings that had started when you were young," he said firmly.

Her parents exchanged a look of surprise when Dawn shook her head and crossed to the porch railing. She placed her hands on the wood as if it would give her the support she required.

"I'm not sure, Pa. Marc is a good man, but there is a difference in him now," she said with her back still to them.

"Of course there is, girl. You just wait and see. He will be around. Now, there will be no more discussion. Florence will allow Arnold's attentions. Then I will decide if I will grant her hand." Alan saw the apprehension return to Dawn's and Richard's faces, and he softened a bit. "I will observe all actions carefully."

Dawn told her parents and Richard goodnight and then made her way to the bedroom where she found her youngest sister asleep and Florence sitting, still dressed. The troubled, smoky eyes lifted to meet her concerned, sapphire ones. She sat down beside her, placing a comforting arm around her. Florence laid her head on her sister's slightly higher shoulder as tears began to course down her cheeks in a small trickle.

"Oh, Dawn, how will I ever do this? I don't think I want to get married, and I know I don't want to marry Arnold."

The tears were now falling in earnest, and despair echoed in her words.

"Shh, shh, Florey, honey. I know how you feel about Arnold, but maybe you should give him a chance. Maybe it will—"

"No," Florence cut her off as she lifted her head and shifted to face her. "I know that I feel terrible when I am with him. That won't change. He is like a vulture! Matt didn't come home, and he is taking advantage. I wish he had gone to war instead of Matt," she bit out.

"Florence, that is a hateful thing to say. Besides, Arnold was too young to go," chided Dawn.

"I know, but Matt was just one year older. He was only thirteen when he left. Matt shouldn't have died. He was only fifteen, just fifteen." Her gaze softened as she recalled the dark-headed youth: his shy brown eyes and soft-spoken ways. "Dawn, from the earliest times I can remember, he was there, watching out for me. The older boys did too, but in a different way. Matt looked deeper. He always knew if I was acting mad because my feelings were hurt or if I was just plain mad. He understood and never made fun of me. Marc always called me his shadow, but he didn't realize I wasn't trailing him. Matt always admired Marc's boldness and wanted to be like him. He and John were always quieter; their parents are just that way. Anyway, Matt was really Marc's shadow, and I was trailing Matt. I quit going fishing with them right before the war started because, for some reason I did not understand at the time, I started acting silly and getting embarrassed whenever I was around Matt. He was my best friend. Sometimes I wished he was my brother instead of Richard because he didn't tease me. Then suddenly, at age eleven, I was glad he wasn't my brother. I was too young to fully understand it. I didn't like acting like a silly girl around him. Now I wish ... " She paused and looked down as she quietly said, "I wish he was here."

Dawn didn't know what to say. Her sister had never confided in her this much. Alice talked all the time. Florence had always been more moody and selective with what she shared. What should she say? Then she thought about Marc.

"Florey, you don't know that Matt would have asked for your hand when he came home. The war changed people. And even if he had, you don't know if you would have wanted to."

Florence started to interrupt, but Dawn held up a hand.

"You may think you know, but you don't. Besides, it was not meant to be. God allowed the war, and he called Matt to heaven."

"I don't understand why," Florence said. She laid her head on Dawn's shoulder again.

Dawn reached up to gently stroke her sister's hair.

"No, I don't either, but we don't have to. Remember in the book of Job in our Bible reading last week when God answered Job? God made and controls everything. Who are we to question whatever he allows?"

Florence sighed heavily and nodded as Dawn continued. "Trust him in this with Arnold. Pa has not consented to a marriage, only courting." She smiled and nudged Florey's head up until she was looking at her. "You are not doomed yet, so let's see a smile."

"You think we can pretend I'm sick for a week

and delay this courting?" Florence asked, a small smile beginning.

Her sister shook her head. "No, sorry. I think Ma and Pa would know."

Florence sighed again. "Very well, let's go to sleep," she said resignedly. "Thank you, Dawn."

They hugged then dressed for bed and blew out the lantern.

∽

The wagon wheels creaked loudly as the Cushman family made their way to town. The familiar sound seemed louder due to the unusual quietness of the wagon's passengers. Even Alice was silent.

It was a relief to finally arrive at church. They filed into the small, white log building and took their seats. Florence slowly looked around the familiar building where she had attended school during the week and church service on Sundays her entire life, the large, rock fireplace that warmed them when it was cold. She gazed out of the window beside her, recalling the many schoolyard games. Suddenly she felt like a grown woman. Childhood was really gone, and she had to let go and move forward.

The sound of more people arriving distracted her from her somber thoughts, and she looked behind her to see who it was. The Wilkins and Johnson families were taking their seats, and not without stirring up excitement. Their neighbors and township were enthusiastically welcoming home their native sons who had finally returned.

Finally, their pastor made his way to the front of the building.

"Good Morning! I see God has sent us wonderful blessings. John Wilkins and Marcus Johnson are home. I know all of you join me in welcoming them. Now, let us praise the Lord in song."

They sang four songs before the message was brought. Florence's focus was not complete until that point. The scripture was from Jeremiah 29:11–14. It concerned the exiled children of Israel. God had plans for a hopeful future for them. The magnitude of God's love settled on Florence. He had positive plans for his children even in the midst of and following adversity.

She looked around to see several tear-stained faces. The war and its devastation would be overcome.

The pastor went on to say, "Just as the Lord had plans for a hopeful future for Israel, so does he have plans for our nation and each of us individually. He wants us to seek him with all our hearts. Let us pray."

During the prayer, the message became even more personal to Florence. He wanted a hopeful future for her, too. She would pray diligently, knowing that when the time came she would be able to be clear where Arnold was concerned. Even though she was still a little apprehensive, she was suddenly more peaceful.

Everyone filed out slowly and shook the pastor's hand. Once out in the yard, Florence made her way to the wagon and was just about to crawl up onto the seat when she saw Arnold making his way toward her. She sighed and waited for him to reach her.

"Good afternoon, Miss Cushman. I'm sure your pa has informed you of his given consent." He waited for her acknowledgment, which came in the form of a nod before continuing. "That being the case, I would like to inform you of my intention of calling on you tomorrow evening."

He looked so formal and earnest. Florence forced herself not to smile. "Very well, Arn ... Mr. Beasley. May I ask what time to expect you?"

"Would after supper be convenient?" he returned.

"Yes, I will prepare some refreshments for our visit. Thank you."

She forced herself to smile politely.

He tipped his hat and turned to join his parents and sisters, who were waiting in their wagon. Mr. and Mrs. Beasley nodded at Florence, and she inclined her head toward them. They had always seemed so serious and stern; Florence had never really spoken with them other than in passing. Now she knew she would be getting to know them better. It seemed strange and very unnerving.

The Beasleys departed, and yet she still stood staring into the space where their wagon had been. Richard startled her as he touched her shoulder, and she visibly jumped. Normally, this would have brought a smile to his face. Not now. Instead he frowned and reached out to gather her close in a brief hug.

"Sorry, Florey, I didn't mean to sneak up on you."

He pulled back to look her in the face. "I'm really sorry."

She made a face at his serious look.

"I'm fine. You didn't frighten me that badly," she said as she pushed away from him and started to climb up into the wagon.

He placed a restraining hand on her arm.

"No, I mean about you having to court Arnold," he explained.

She stepped back down and looked up at him.

"Oh." She paused thoughtfully. "Well, the preacher said God has a hopeful future for us, all of us, if we seek him. So, brother, I am going to be an obedient daughter and not bring embarrassment on Ma and Pa, and ... I will pray for the Lord's will and wait and see."

"Well, well, little Florey is growing up. I'm not sure I am ready. Just remember, I'm in your corner. If you discover Arnold is not the one for you, I'll stand beside you," Richard said firmly and then mumbled, "I'm doubly obligated."

Florence smiled and then looked puzzled at the last. "What do you mean, 'Doubly obligated'? How?"

Richard started backing and stammered, "No-nothing. Forget I said anything, really, sis."

She put her hands on her hips in an all too familiar stubborn gesture.

He threw up his hands in surrender and sighed deeply before he answered, "Matt."

Tears filled her eyes, and they deepened with emotion. Florence saw surprise register on his face.

Her brother removed his hat, ran a hand through his hair, and turned toward the wagon. He hung his arms over the sides and looked down. She could tell he was gathering his thoughts. The last couple of days had proven very hard. She placed a hand on his shoulder, light as a feather, for a moment then propped on the wagon beside him and waited. He turned his head and met her dusky eyes.

"I told you about the promise I made Matt about John. Well, he also made a request of me as your brother. There wasn't much time. He sent his ma and pa his love and asked them not to be sad. Then, what you know he said about John. Then the last thing he said surprised me and reached deep into my gut. He said, 'Florey, tell Florey I love her, and … make sure she marries someone who loves her.' Florence …" Richard trailed off helplessly as he saw the tears spilling unheeded down his sister's face.

Suddenly she turned and hugged him so hard it unsteadied him.

She gave him a watery smile. "Thank you, more than you'll ever know. Now, no matter what, I know a special boy loved me. That is something that can never be taken from me. Matt Wilkins loved me, and although he never knew for sure, I loved him. With as much as was in my young heart, and it is still there."

A soft voice caused her to turn. "He knew, my

dear. He knows now." Mrs. Wilkins gently held out her arms, and Florence went into them.

Her parents, Dawn, and Alice arrived at that moment, all with bewildered looks. Her ma placed a hand on her shoulder, and Florence turned, wiping her cheeks.

"Florence, whatever is it? I saw Arnold talking to you. Has he decided to withdraw his request?" Ella Cushman asked.

It seemed so impossible that her ma still could not see the truth of the matter. Yet she had never been one to confide much to her ma. Dawn and Alice were much easier for her ma to understand. She had always wanted to be outdoors when she was supposed to be indoors. There had been more than one petticoat ripped climbing a tree.

"No, ma'am. Arnold will be calling on me tomorrow evening. We were just talking about Matt's last moments with Richard," she answered.

Florence shot an imploring look at Richard not to elaborate. She saw Dawn catch the look and knew someone would have to explain things to her at some point.

"I am so sorry my son has caused you to relive your pain, Mary," Ella said sympathetically.

"Oh, not at all, Ella. It brings me comfort to know all I can. Richard being with him has been one of my greatest comforts, and Florence, well, you know how fond we are of her. We had hoped ... "

Florence caught her father watching the

exchanges in silence. He moved forward and took her hands.

"Florence, since your brother has caused such a stirring of emotions, the least we can do is to send you home with Mrs. Wilkins for the day. I know, it being Sunday, you won't be able to help with any work, but it would be allowed to give her comfort if she is so inclined as to have you," Alan Cushman said gruffly.

His wife started to protest, but he silenced her with a look.

Florence's eyes flew to Mrs. Wilkins' kind face. No emotions were displayed there. Florence held her breath. She would love to spend the afternoon at the Wilkins' farm. If days had been counted, she probably had spent almost as much time there while growing up as she had on her family's farm.

A controlled smile of acceptance had now appeared on Mrs. Wilkins' face. "We would love to have Florence. John, Boyd, and Carl have matters they plan to discuss this afternoon, so I will value the company. Thank you."

"It's settled then. Florence, I'll come for you before supper time."

Alan turned and began assisting his wife and other daughters into the wagon. They would go to Richard and Jenny's for lunch and then home. He settled on the buckboard seat and slapped the reins.

Richard gave Florence a final look, nodded to Mary, and spoke briefly with Carl and John as he passed them on his way to rescue Jenny, who had been cornered by the town's gossip. Everyone had seen John and Marc with him yesterday, and Erma Scott was probably trying to find out the details.

❧

Marcus Johnson stood leaning against the church building and had watched the events beside the Cushman's wagon in fascination. He gathered from Arnold's formal approach what had transpired. He was still incredulous that Mr. Cushman had agreed. However, the rest perplexed him even more. What could Richard have told Florence that would have brought such tears?

A grimace was on his face as his mother finished talking to the pastor and came to stand in front of him.

"Son, what a serious face for such a beautiful day! Did your father give up on me?" She glanced around and then back at her son.

He grinned. "Yeah, he took my horse. He said you would talk past lunch! I really think he just wanted to try my mustang. Did you finish your planning?"

"Yes," she said in a slightly smug tone, and her eyes twinkled.

"Ma, what have you planned?"

She turned and walked toward the wagon where Will and Jack were waiting. They were pulling at the necks of their Sunday shirts and looked not just a little impatient. They eagerly clambered into the wagon at the approach of their mother and brother.

"Marc, can we go now?" Jack whined.

86 ~ LANA LYNNE

"Yeah, I gotta get these shoes off," added Will.

Marc ignored them and focused on his mother, who was now smiling gleefully. "Ma, would you please forewarn me of the plans you have made?"

His brothers' attentions were instantly diverted from their complaints.

"What plans?" they inquired in unison.

Emily looked at the attentive faces of her sons and sighed in enjoyment. She smiled at her eldest son.

"Help me into the wagon, and I'll tell you all about it on the way home."

Marcus gladly assisted her. He clearly recalled his mother's delight in planning surprises. It was with well-earned concern, sprinkled with a still-intact sense of humor that he settled onto the seat beside her and picked up the reins. He glanced at her out of the corner of his eye as the horses started forward and waited.

They were halfway home before she spoke.

"Oh dear, I was supposed to tell you boys about something, wasn't I? Now what could it have been?"

"Ma, what is it?" Jack and Will asked in unison.

"Please, Ma."

"Ma, you remember."

She smiled and held up a silencing hand.

"The pastor and I were discussing the possibility of a town social to welcome Marc and John home. We think it will be a good time for the town. All these new people are passing through; it would help the town get together for a nice evening to remind the ones who were here first that we have not forgotten who we were before the war. The one thing that is a little concerning is whether we will be able to procure or should even try to procure Mr. Ward to provide the music. He is so wonderful on the violin, especially when he plays 'The Arkansas Traveler,' but some people have mixed feelings about his work. As the war is over, I don't mind. What do you think, Marc?"

Marc smiled at the excitement on his mother's face. It was so nice to know that his coming home had freed her to be the way he always remembered her. His mother loved to make plans and do things for the community but especially for the ones she loved. His brothers had told him that she had really stayed away from town, except for Sundays, since the war began. He would not deny her this. Even if he had to put up with all the stares and gossip that he knew would be present. Heck, he would even dance with Thelma Mason, who always stepped on your feet, if it brought a smile to his mother's face.

"I say we will need a dandy fiddle player. If Mr. Ward is available, great!"

His brothers were already arguing over who would take Alice.

His mother turned to them. "Why don't you both take her?" This settled it, and she turned and smiled at Marc. "Thank you."

A lump formed in Marc's throat, and he swallowed hard. "Oh, Ma, it's just a party. I—"

Her hand covered his, and she looked directly

88 ~ LANA LYNNE

into his eyes. "No, son, I mean, thank you for coming home."

He felt moisture form in his eyes and answered softly, "Yes, ma'am." He turned and focused on the road, slapping the reins to increase their pace a bit.

As they passed by the Wilkins' farm, Marc observed John helping his ma and Florence from their buckboard. Carl came out with Boyd, and then in an almost tandem motion, their attention returned to the road. A brisk breeze suddenly blew, causing a spiral of leaves to fall from the trees overhanging the road. Dust blew slightly in their faces, causing Will and John to sputter and blink their eyes. Marc pulled his hat down farther on his head and chuckled.

"What's so funny?" asked Jack.

"It just reminded me of driving cattle in Texas. Suddenly I tried to picture my two little brothers in a real dirt storm. You can't see your own hand in front of you at times," Marc replied with a smile.

"If you could do it, so could we," Will boasted.

"You're welcome to—," Marc stopped as his mother caught his eye in a warning and imploring look, "explore that when you are much older." He couldn't believe that he had almost asked his brothers to go back to Texas with him. Sometimes he could be so insensitive.

He was relieved to pull up to their barn. His brothers jumped out and were on the porch before he could climb down and come around to assist their mother from the wagon. His pa opened the door and was almost stampeded as the boys ran past him.

HOME ALWAYS BECKONS ~ 89

"Whoa, you boys slow down and walk."

Lee Johnson pulled both youths back by their shirtbacks.

"Yes, Pa," they both answered and were released. Then they quickly walked inside.

Lee turned toward the yard. "Marc, that animal of yours is real fine. It didn't take long to get home."

"Lee Johnson! You didn't race home on the Lord's day, did you?" Emily Johnson exhaled her breath as Marc lifted her to the ground.

"Yes, Emily, I did. The Lord made that fine beast, and I just rejoiced in the discovery," returned her husband unabashedly.

Lee winked at Marc. Emily hid her own smile by looking down to dust off dirt the road wind had deposited on the skirt of her dress. Marc grinned and began unhitching the horses. His ma moved across the yard and onto the porch where his pa stood holding the door for her. They disappeared inside.

His parents' love had always been evident to him and his brothers. They had been blessed. Growing up he had seen the parents of his friends. For some reason he had watched their interactions. Some had shown tolerance and duty, other's quiet, strong love with hardly any overt verbal mentions or displays, and many varied relationships. As a child he never judged what relationships were "supposed to be" or if the couples were happy. He only knew that most of the time, watching his parents' exchanges made him happy. That was his measuring stick. To him, theirs was the most harmonious balance, even when they disagreed, because they kept their senses of humor. He hoped to have that kind of relationship one day.

He led the horses into the barn. After he finished tending them, he made his way to the house. His ma had sat out the lunch, which had been mostly prepared the day before, and they were waiting for him. He apologized for the delay in joining them as he slid into place. Grace was said and the meal proceeded. Topics of conversation ranged from farm crops to the still changing Arkansas leadership and government. Arkansas was not a state again. The information they had led them to believe that many of the southern states governments would be declared illegal soon. There was also talk of forming military districts out of those states. If that happened, there was apprehension about who would be sent to command their district. Speculation was great, and his pa pointed out that few facts were available. Therefore, the conversation moved to the pastor's sermon. His message of hope was one they all needed.

Lee patted his stomach.

"Thank you for a wonderful meal, Emily. I suggest we excuse ourselves."

He stood and made his way to the mantle and reached for his pipe. Marc loved the familiar routine. His brothers disappeared outside.

Marc stood up and surprised his ma by assisting her with clearing the plates.

"Marcus, this is woman's work," she said, taking the plates from his hand and placing them beside the water bucket where she would rinse them.

HOME ALWAYS BECKONS ~ 91

"Ma, there aren't any women out on the range with the cattle. I've cooked and rinsed my own dishes."

"Land sakes, Son, you do continue to amaze me." She smiled and did not protest as he helped her spread the cloth over the remaining food on the table. They would uncover it at supper time. They shared a smile, and just as he was about to turn away, her words stopped him.

"Florence has always been close to the Wilkins. I never really realized it until after Matt died. Mary and I became closer with our sons away from home. It seems that Florence tagged along behind and beside Matt almost from the day she could walk."

Marc shook his head.

"John said that Matt had really cared for Florence, and their parents had hoped they would marry. Call me blind, but that idea never crossed my mind. To me, they were both 'my two little shadows.'"

His ma's eyebrows shot up. "Thinking a little highly of yourself weren't you, Son?"

He frowned slightly. "I guess I was. So, Florence's hero was Matt?"

She nodded and waited for the significance of what they had seen today register on her son. It took a moment. Then he looked up, and she saw the grief and understanding.

"They're closing the door on what might have been. Now that Mr. Cushman has obviously agreed to Arnold calling on Florence, they have to let it all go," he stated.

The focus was shifting from his perspective to that of others. He had been through so much, and the tendency was to tighten the circle of self-protection. Now the circle was broadening. She nodded her head in response. Marc turned and made his way to where his pa was sitting.

Chapter
Five

The remainder of October passed, and November began with a continuing mixture of subtle changes. Florence and Arnold had settled into a routine. Every Monday evening after supper, he would come to call. The conversation usually started with the weather and ended with Arnold's narrative of how things would be when they were married. Florence would listen quietly and comment when appropriate or when asked, which was hardly ever. Her pa would come out onto the porch at eight o'clock, and Arnold would bid them goodnight. Florence would hug her pa and go into bed.

There was another member of their family who also now had a regular routine. Dawn had accompanied her to visit Mary Wilkins one day. They had arrived close to lunch time. Mary was about to take lunch out to Carl, John, and Boyd, who were working on a new well. They had walked with her, and the men were very glad to see them when they arrived. On the way back to the Wilkins' house, Dawn had

HOME ALWAYS BECKONS ~ 95

made several polite inquiries about Mr. Richards. Florence recalled Dawn's horror over what she had shared with her about Boyd's wife and child. That day Dawn had volunteered to come by a couple of days a week and take the men their lunch so Mrs. Wilkins and Florence could visit. They usually visited while washing or mending.

The township had also been anticipating the social event that Mrs. Johnson and several of the ladies had been able to organize. It was to be the second Friday of the month. Florence sighed as she finished milking the cow. It was now only a day away. This event would officially announce to the town that Arnold Beasley and Florence Cushman were, for all purposes, close to being engaged. She paused and sent another prayer for guidance upward.

She had tried to do everything in the appropriate manner; her parents seemed satisfied. Arnold's parents even went out of their way to speak to her and her family at church. Arnold had behaved very respectfully. Still, Florence wasn't comfortable with him or the arrangement. He had started giving her hand a brief kiss as he bid her and her pa goodnight. Everything in her wanted to snatch her hand away and demand that he leave her alone. She knew she would get more comfortable in time; at least that was what she had been told by her ma.

"There, there, Ol' Rob." She soothed the cow, which had become restless.

She patted the soft hair of their milk cow. She remembered when the calf had been born. They had called her Little Robin. Now she was Ol' Rob. How fast the time had passed.

Florence smiled ruefully. It was funny. When she was a little girl she had thought time passed so slowly. You would anticipate things, and they never seemed to happen soon enough. She and Dawn couldn't wait to grow up. Now that they were grown, she wished they could slow things down a bit. But not Alice. She shook her head as she thought of her little sister. She was still trying to rush life to hurry up and happen.

Florence finished filling the milk bucket, stood up, and placed the stool in the corner of the stall. She started toward the house, but stopped as her eyes beheld the sunrise, golden threads reaching through the charcoal sky like the flame in a lantern, which flickers initially, sending out only small breaks in the darkness, but as the wick is turned higher, it burns brighter and brighter until it illuminates a room. In a much more glorious display, the sun would continue to reemerge from the darkness, and the bright day would arrive. She sighed. A new sunrise—a new day. Hope was there.

She looked upward and said, "Thank you, Lord." Now, with her dismal thoughts gone, she continued to the house.

The smell of eggs in the skillet permeated her nose as she opened the door. Dawn had gathered them earlier. Alice was setting the plates on the table. Her ma came to take the bucket of milk from her.

"Florey, I thought I was going to have to send Alice after you. What took you so long?" Ella Cushman asked her middle child. She poured the milk into a large pitcher as she waited for a reply. None came, and she stopped, putting a hand on her hip and turning toward her daughter. "Florence Elizabeth, I am waiting for an answer."

Florence shifted uncomfortably. She didn't want to elaborate on her thoughts of the morning, but she wanted to be truthful. Finally, she looked up at her mother. "I'm sorry, Ma. I was thinking about the social tomorrow night, and it made me work a little slower."

Her mother's frown turned into a smile. "I know you must be excited! Dawn and I finished sewing the trim on your dresses. It was so nice of Miss O'Neal to let us have the fabric for such a small price. She said it was left over from before the war, and she needed to sell it to make room for the new shipment that had come in on the ferry. It is the first new shipment she's had since the war."

Dawn and Florence exchanged looks. Florence knew Dawn understood that her feelings about the dance were anything but excited.

"I think my dress turned out to be the prettiest of them all. It is the loveliest shade of green. Will and Jack will be so pleased," Alice said dreamily.

Florence stepped to her little sister and fingered a golden strand of the hair she still wore flowing down her back. "You will be the most beautiful belle of all."

Alan Cushman entered at that moment, and all

98 ~ LANA LYNNE

were quickly seated. He liked to have breakfast on time so he could begin his day's work.

"Alice and Dawn, you will be riding into town with me this morning. I need to get some lumber to replace that rotten place in the barn. I'll drop you off at school. Dawn, don't forget to check on Jenny. Florence will stay here today and help Ma."

Dawn had been teaching half days, as the regular teacher had been very ill. Mrs. Nettle had returned to the classroom, but tired easily; therefore, she only came for the last few hours in the early afternoon.

Breakfast ended, and her pa, Dawn, and Alice left for town. Florence helped her ma with the dishes and then the churning. The morning passed with more chores and baking. She could tell that her mother had really made a special effort lately in helping her develop the skills she would need to be a wife who took good care of her home.

∾

After lunch Florence asked her ma if she could go for a walk, and her mother agreed. She sighed deeply. She seemed to be doing a lot of that lately. As she reached her special spot beside the grouping of trees on the hill, she felt the tension ease from her body. She settled in with her back against the large tree trunk and closed her eyes.

A smile danced about her lips, and a slight blush crept on her face as she remembered the last time she had spoken with Matt. It had been the day before the company had marched away from Rockport. She had been sitting in this very spot. Her eyes had been closed, as now, and she had suddenly felt a tickle on her cheek. She had wiped at her cheek as her eyes opened to find twinkling brown eyes gazing down at her. There had been Matt with a leaf in his hand.

The scene in her memory continued.

"Hey, I thought I might find you here. You know you're too young to be so worried. We all will be back in a few weeks." Matt had paused, seeing her look of uncertainty. "Well, it won't be more than a few months at most. Marc and Richard said so."

He had moved toward her and slumped down beside her. They both had stared into the distance without speaking for a while; then Florence had leaned forward, pulling her knees up under her skirt, and had propped her chin on her knees. She had felt a tug on the single braid that hung down her back and turned her head, laying her cheek on her knee. Matt had been staring at her in a strange and serious way. She saw him swallow hard. Slowly, he had leaned forward and gently touched her nose and cheeks.

"I like your freckles," he said, and then the color rose in his neck, and he pulled his hand away.

Her dove-colored eyes had been wide in her twelve-year-old face.

"Matt, are you feeling all right? You look a little sick. Maybe you shouldn't go tomorrow," she said practically.

He looked up at the limbs hanging above him, trying to gather his thoughts and courage. Florence shifted and started to rise, but he reached for her hand.

"Florey, I wanted to tell you good-bye without all the others around. You are my best friend, and I have started to care about you even more, sort of different lately. Do you know what I mean?"

Florence had hesitated and then sunk to her knees beside him. She had experienced that funny feeling in her stomach, which had made her uncomfortable to be around him. She had never been uncomfortable around him until a few months prior to that day. Her stomach had started to flutter whenever he was near, and she couldn't speak without stammering. She had not liked it. He had been Matt, her best friend. She didn't understand those feelings at the time. But suddenly, as he had sat there looking at her with those gentle, colt-like eyes, she realized her feelings were nothing to hide.

She looked at him shyly on that day. "Yes, I do. Matt, I will miss you."

Then in almost a whisper, he asked, "May I kiss you good-bye?"

She had nodded without speaking. He leaned forward and briefly, softly touched his lips to hers. They opened their eyes simultaneously, sharing the wonder of their very first kiss.

"I'll be back soon," he had promised.

"I'll be here," she replied.

He jumped up and ran up the hill. As he reached the top, he turned and shouted, "Wave to me tomorrow."

The next day she had waved as he, his brother, her father, her brother, Marc, and the men and boys she had known her whole life marched past.

She had kept her promise. She was still here, but Matt...

"Matt, you promised to be back soon. You promised. If you had come back, I wouldn't have to put up with Arnold," Florence said out loud.

The sound of her words suddenly made her ashamed. It wasn't Matt's fault. It just was. She looked up remorsefully and prayed.

"Dear God, I'm sorry. Please tell Matt I love him and miss him. I know you're taking care of him. And please help me to do what is right by Ma and Pa and Arnold. Thank you. In Jesus' name, amen."

The wind, which now held a slight chill, blew across her face. She was glad for the long sleeves of her cotton day dress. She stood, smoothing the full beige skirt. Gathering the length slightly with one hand, she began to climb the hill.

Florence reached the top, turned, and looked back one last time, drinking in the peaceful view of the trees and pond before continuing on her way home. As she disappeared over the crest of the hill, a solitary figure stepped from behind a tree midway down the hill. John had been on his way to see her when he heard her speak. Her words had stunned him, and he had quickly stepped behind the tree. Then her prayer had brought tears to his eyes. Until a few months ago, he had not truly understood the power of prayer. When he had finally surrendered everything to the Lord, peace had come. He had grown up with Florence being around, but he had never really talked to her much—but Matt had. Matt had never been much of a talker to anybody else, except for his family and Florence. Until this moment, he had not remembered that Matt and Florence had been baptized in the river on the same Sunday about a year before the war started. He looked down at the small square, calico-wrapped package in his hands. His mother had insisted that he take it to Florence when she brought them lunch. He wasn't sure what was in it, but he was pretty sure he could guess.

He stroked the soft fabric with his thumbs; then, letting go with one hand, he ran the other through his dark hair. He took a deep breath, shook his head, and started after Florence. He reached her just as she reached the corner of the back of her house.

"Florence," called John.

She turned, and her skirt made a slight rustle. Amber hair swept into a knot at the base of her neck, the familiar single plait from long ago gone. The freckles had faded until only a few were barely present across the bridge of her nose. The cheeks that had been slightly full were now slimmed by high cheekbones. He would have loved to have seen Matt's expression if he could have seen her.

"John, how nice to see you!" She smiled pleasantly. A look of concern suddenly crossed her face. "Is something wrong?"

"No, no. Ma just wanted me to bring you this."

He awkwardly held out the package.

She glanced at the outstretched gift and back to John before taking it.

"Oh, thank you," she said.

He and Matt had always resembled each other. Her gaze lingered on his face as she took the parcel, as if trying to find remnants of his brother there.

"I'd better be getting back. Pa and Boyd will need my help. Good afternoon."

He started to walk past her.

"John, would you mind staying while I open it? I want to be able to tell your ma how I liked whatever it is," she requested softly.

They both somehow knew it had to do with Matt. She did not want to be alone when she opened it.

He nodded and said, "Of course."

Slowly she untied the ribbon, which held the blue calico fabric in place. Her hand trembled as she removed the soft covering to reveal a photograph. Her breath caught in her throat. Mrs. Wilkins had told her she had received two pictures of John and Matt in their uniforms that had never been shown to anyone. She had put them away and vowed to only take them out when her boys came home. Florence turned the picture over; it was dated 1863.

"That was taken before Gettysburg. One of those men that came around and took pictures, he even took pictures of things after the battles. Oh, I'm sorry, that was not an appropriate thing to say. May I?" asked John as he reached out a hand, and Florence placed the picture in his hand. He stared at it for a moment, memories racing. "That's how he looked the last time I saw him. Marc and I were taken prisoner and well... You know what happened."

He handed the picture back to her.

She stroked the picture and looked back at John. She saw the differences. John's face was squarer; she could see from the picture that Matt's face had become more angular and long. Both were tall, but John's shoulders were broader. She liked the more angular, slender build of Matt. He would have matured well, but it had not been meant. The image she had held was now updated from a thirteen-year-old to a fifteen-year-old, but the physical form of the boy she had known would not change anymore. He was frozen in time. Understanding of why Mrs. Wilkins had sent this now came. Florence had to let go of what might have been. No matter what, she had this to remind her of how her most special friend had looked. Once again, the message that it was time to put away the things of childhood was conveyed.

She clasped the photo to the bodice of her dress and squared her shoulders as she looked up at the man who could have been her brother-in-law if Matt had lived.

"John, please thank your ma. If she ever wants it back, I will bring it. Tell her I understand. And John, thank you for staying while I opened it. I'm sorry to cause you pain," she said softly.

"I'll tell her. Florence, in a way, it helped me too. Thank you for letting me stay as you opened it. If you ever need anything, please let me know. In a way I'll always be like another brother to you." He nodded at her. "Good afternoon."

"Good afternoon, John."

❧

Her ma was sitting at the table with their ball gowns draped beside her. She glanced at the item Florence clasped to her heart.

"I gather John Wilkins found you. You are getting too old to be disappearing to that old place. It isn't proper for a young woman. What did he bring you?'

"A picture of Matt." She hesitated briefly before handing it to her mother.

Ella's lips pressed into a firm line as she returned the photograph.

"I do not understand her purpose. Arnold would certainly not approve of your having that. It can do nothing but come between you," she said.

"It won't if he doesn't know about it," Florence said softly.

Her ma looked shocked. "You don't mean to be a secretive wife? That can only bring strife. I'll not have my daughter behaving in such a manner. You will tell him or I shall."

"Ma, please don't do that. He has not even officially asked for my hand. This has nothing to do with him," Florence pleaded.

"Florence, after tomorrow night I am sure it will only be a short time before you officially become engaged. I am only thinking of your future. You will tell him, and that is all I have to say. Now, help me finish the trim on the gowns for the dance. The Yankees may have ravaged our plantations and farms, but our daughters are still going to look lovely."

Ella was firm and looked down at her needle work, missing the slight tremble of her daughter's chin as she sat across from her.

～

The rest of the afternoon passed with the completing of the finishing touches. All the gowns were made from the same pattern with the appropriate adjustments for their varied measurements. However, the fabrics were all different. Mrs. O'Neal had ten varied fabrics, which she had hidden under the boards of the store floor during the war. She had almost forgotten them until she heard about the social, and her quick ability to cipher amounts for profit, allowing discounts for the depleted finances of her neighbors, had prevailed. All were purchased by different families the day she had announced their availability. None of the women had been allowed the opportunity of new clothing since the war. The river trade had been halted for all functional purposes during those years.

The skirts and bodices were separate pieces made from matching fabrics. The bodices had slightly off-the-shoulder necklines, short puffed sleeves, and had sharp pointed waistbands. The skirts were long, full, and gathered to a banded waist, which fit snugly under the bodice. Dawn's dress was yellow taffeta brocade with a green diamond print, which her ma had trimmed with beige lace at the sleeves and neckline. Florence's dress was pale blue brocade with white ribbon trim at the sleeves. Alice's dress was slightly shorter due to her age and was heavy green cotton. Mrs. Cushman had also modified the neckline with a beige lace undershirt, which would cover Alice's neck, shoulders, and chest. The dresses were all lined with white polished cotton. Mrs. Cushman had fashioned the girls' petticoats from old nightgowns that they had outgrown. She was distressed that they weren't crinoline. She also wished she had boning for the bodices.

Alice and Dawn came home mid-afternoon and began making supper while Florence and Ella finished the garments. Once the task was completed, the treasured pieces were carefully put away in anticipation of the activities of the next day. The table was then set, and still Alan Cushman did not arrive. Finally, Ella had them all sit down and began the meal without him. They were halfway finished when he opened the door. He took off his hat and hung it on the nail behind the door. He then crossed to the table and sat in his place.

"Ella, I am sorry to be late. There was a matter of much importance Carl and John Wilkins had to discuss with me." He held up a hand as Ella started to speak. His glance encompassed their daughters before returning to his wife. "We will discuss it later."

"Yes, Alan," his wife responded with a slightly resentful tone.

The meal and cleanup activities complete, the girls bade their parents goodnight and made their way to their bedroom.

The next morning dawned with an air of excitement. Chores were completed quicker and moods were lighter. After lunch, the preparations for the evening's social event began. Alan Cushman tried to stay out of the way of the bustling women folk in his house. About an hour before they would leave, he went in and put on his Sunday coat and pants. Ella had dug out a dress she had packed away that one of her cousins in Virginia had sent her before the war. She had never had the opportunity to wear it. It was ivory silk taffeta brocade with a crinoline petticoat. She felt badly about wearing it, but her daughters had stated how proud they would be to see her in it. After helping the girls finish their preparations, she had rushed to get dressed. When she emerged, she felt almost like a school girl again. Alan rose with an appreciative gleam in his eye, one she had not seen in years. The girls stared, and Dawn's eyes were moist as a wide smile beamed at her mother.

"Ma, you look so beautiful," Dawn said, crossing to take her hands.

Alice and Florence nodded in agreement.

"I am so honored to have you on my arm this night," Alan said, crossing to offer his arm.

His wife's golden hair, which now held highlights of gray, was accented by a single silver comb under the softly coiled bun at the crown of her head. The blue eyes held a sparkle he had not seen in a while. The lines at the corners of her eyes and mouth just seemed to add to her beauty. This was the woman who had worked beside him and with him all these years. She had become tougher; she had to with the farming life they lived. He remembered the privileged young lady he had met in Virginia all those years ago. She had been pampered and spoiled but was the loveliest thing he had ever seen. He had loved her after she had snubbed him following their first meeting, and then had rushed to talk to him after her parents had been out of sight. What spunk she had and what love. She had given up a life of wealth and comfort to marry him. Suddenly he realized how much he had begun to take for granted.

"Forgive me?" he bent and whispered in her ear.

"Whatever for, Alan?" she asked in confusion.

"For forgetting to tell you what a wonderful and beautiful woman you are every day," he replied softly, but their daughters heard and turned away, smiling.

She blushed and then frowned. "Oh, Alan, what kind of talk is that?" Then she smiled softly. "Thank you."

A knock was heard at the door. Ella moved forward and opened it, expecting to find only Arnold. Instead there was Arnold calling for Florence, as well as Will and Jack calling for Alice. Ella graciously asked them into the house. Will and Jack,

110 ~ LANA LYNNE

with mouths gaping, rushed to help Alice gather her wrap and gloves. They escorted her to the buckboard, where Mr. and Mrs. Johnson were waiting, as if she were the queen of England. Florence and Arnold's departure was much quieter and more proper. Her parents promised to see them at the dance.

Arnold glanced over at her every now and then as he guided the horses toward town. Finally, he spoke as they began to see the bright lights comprised of many candles and lanterns surrounding the wooden dance floor, which had been built for the event in the center of town in front of the courthouse.

"Florence, I think we should discuss my expectations for this evening," he said.

"Yes, Arnold?" She turned to face him as he pulled the buggy in line with the others at the edge of the church.

"As tonight will let everyone see you are spoken for, I expect you to act in an appropriate manner. I must give my permission before you may dance with anyone except me. Is that understood?" he said firmly.

Florence stared at him in stunned silence. This is what it would be like if she married him. She would have to ask his permission before she could do anything. The request he had made was not unreasonable, but it was the way in which he said it. It was at that moment she remembered what her ma had told her she must do.

"Very well, Arnold. Also, there is something I

should tell you. Mrs. Wilkins has given me a picture of Matt for me to keep."

It was Arnold's turn to look stunned. His face changed in a way Florence had never seen. It was a look of pure rage. He grabbed her by her upper arms and shook her.

"You will give it back immediately, do you understand? You showed me a lack of respect to accept it. Matthew Wilkins is no longer in your life or anybody else's. Even if he were here, he would not be allowed to have you. I decided that long ago. He would never even let me near you, even as children. Now he has no say. Florence, do you understand?" he shouted.

Florence could feel his fingers biting into her upper arms and nodded as tears stung her eyes. Still he did not release her.

"Say it. I want you to tell me what you are going to do," he said in lower, measured tones.

Florence heard a horse approaching. Arnold released her and turned to look at the approaching rider. As the horse neared, Florence could see that it was Marcus Johnson's mustang.

Arnold turned to her and whispered, "You are not to speak of this."

Marc reined his horse beside his parents' wagon, which was two wagons away from Arnold's. Florence prayed he would come over and speak. She didn't want to be out here alone with Arnold anymore.

As they waited for Marc to dismount, their attention stayed focused in his direction. They did not notice the tall figure in a blue uniform approaching the wagon on Florence's side. Suddenly a gruff, deep voice startled them.

"Is there a problem here, ma'am?" the man addressed Florence.

Florence glanced at Arnold.

The man looked from the obviously distressed young woman to the young man beside her.

"I heard loud, angry shouting, and as I am one of the soldiers making sure there are no problems tonight, it is my duty to investigate."

Before Florence could answer, Marcus, who had made his way to the wagon, spoke. "Good evening, Florence and Arnold. Did I hear this lieutenant say there was shouting? It couldn't have been you."

Arnold squeezed her hand hard in warning.

"Well, I had shared some disturbing information with Mr. Beasley, and he was upset. Everything is fine now. Thank you gentlemen for your concern, but I assure you it is unnecessary," she said as calmly as possible.

"Yes, I'm afraid I didn't realize how loud my voice was. I apologize for disturbing the peace. I didn't realize all our social functions would be Union supervised," Arnold confirmed.

If they had been in the light, they would have seen the lieutenant's eyes narrow at Arnold's statement. However, darkness covered his reaction.

His calm reply showed none of his emotions. "As your state has still not been readmitted to the United States, there will be soldiers around periodically until that happens. Now, as everything here appears to be in order, I bid you a pleasant evening." He turned to leave and then stopped, turning toward Marcus. "Sir, I did not get your name."

Marcus stiffened. He had to fight the rush of emotions that had coursed through him at the sight of the officer's hat. He was better, but each time he encountered a blue uniform, a part of him relived the war. "Marcus Johnson."

"Marcus Johnson? You are one of the men they are honoring here tonight." The officer moved toward the man in question.

"Yes, sir, I was Lieutenant Marcus Johnson, third Arkansas regiment." Marcus's voice was strong and full of pride.

"The men of your regiment were tough fighters. My regiment faced yours at one point, but we won't discuss that now. Welcome home, Lieutenant Johnson."

"It is just Mr. Johnson now."

"Enjoy your evening, Mr. Johnson. Oh, there is one thing I would like to discuss with you further." The man turned to Florence and Arnold, who still sat in the buggy. "Why don't you escort your young lady to the festivities? Mr. Johnson and I will only be a moment."

Arnold paused. "May I have your name, sir?"

"Lieutenant Hawkins." He turned his head toward Florence. "Ma'am, please call on me if I can be of assistance at any time."

Arnold climbed out of the buggy and turned to assist Florence. "I assure you, Miss Cushman will not require anyone's assistance but my own. Thank you, Lieutenant Hawkins."

Arnold and Florence made their way toward the lively violin music and laughter. The wooden floor was surrounded by posts from which hung brightly lit lanterns. Florence clutched her soft shawl around her with her white gloved hands as she and Arnold came into the light. Alice spotted her at once and came from the center of the floor with Will in tow.

"I am so glad you are here. We are having such a lovely time, but I was getting worried because Ma, Pa, and Dawn have not yet arrived. Richard and Jenny are over by the refreshments. You were also a long time getting here. Anyway, you're here now. Doesn't William look wonderful all dressed up?"

"Alice, please," pleaded Will with a pained look at being made the center of attention.

"Not as wonderful as me, though? Right, Alice?" Jack grinned as he joined them. "I believe the next dance is mine."

"Excuse us, please." Alice giggled as Jack swept her onto the dance floor.

Florence smiled as Jack stepped on Alice's foot twice within the first few steps. She glanced at Will and could tell he had also seen it. He looked rather smug and satisfied. Then he turned to Florence.

"Miss Florence, may I please have this dance? I promise your shoes will not suffer for their trouble."

She smiled, but then Arnold cleared his throat pointedly.

"Will, I believe this dance is Mr. Beasley's.

Maybe later in the evening if it is all right with Mr. Beasley."

Will graciously said, "I will look forward to it." Then he moved closer to watch Alice and Jack.

Arnold inclined his head toward the dancing couples. "Miss Cushman, shall we?" It was a seemingly polite request, which sounded like a command.

She placed her gloved hand on the arm he offered, and they made their way to the floor. Arnold's dancing was mechanically correct but stilted. They did not speak. Florence scanned the on-looking faces for her parents and Dawn, but they were not there. Finally, as the song ended and they turned to move toward the side of the floor, Dawn's golden hair emerged into the light. She watched, waiting for Mr. Richards to also emerge, but when Dawn's escort came into view, it was John Wilkins! Dawn was smiling up at him so sweetly, and he was looking down with an equally adoring look. Then her parents, Mr. and Mrs. Wilkins, and then Boyd Richards entered behind the couple. Florence was dumbfounded and then severely irritated that no one had told her!

She quickly made her way to her sister with a very displeased Arnold following her. Dawn saw her coming and reached out her hands to clasp her younger sister's.

"Florence, don't look that way. I wanted to tell you, but Pa and John thought it best to wait until tonight. We didn't want to take away from you and Arnold. That's why we took so long to get here. We wanted you to make your entrance first. Forgive us?"

she requested with first an anxious frown and then an imploring smile.

Florence squeezed her sister's hands. "Of course, I'm just surprised." She paused and looked up at John. "May I ask your intentions toward my sister?"

"Florence, I believe I have covered that," her pa interjected and turned to clasp John on the shoulder. "His intentions are so honorable and sure that he has already requested your sister's hand. They will have a courtship, but they would like to officially announce it tonight. Will I have the need to announce another engagement?" He looked pointedly at Arnold and Florence.

He saw his middle daughter's face pale, and he glanced at Arnold.

Arnold drew Florence's hand onto his arm. "It is a little premature at this point, as I have not officially asked her hand. It will be soon. Tonight has shown the town our courtship. Tonight was planned to honor John and Marcus."

"Very well, Arnold. Now, I would like to have the honor of a dance with my wife." Alan turned. "Ella?"

John and Dawn's entrance had caused quite a stir. Not many people had truly been surprised by Arnold and Florence's entrance as a couple. Arnold had been very vocal about his intentions toward Florence Cushman. However, the town had always expected Marcus and Dawn to court, not John and Dawn.

Arnold excused himself to get them some refreshments.

Florence overheard Mrs. Tate, the lawyer's wife, asking, "Who would have thought it? I wonder if that's the reason Marcus Johnson has not arrived. Maybe he is too heartbroken."

"The poor boy, he and John Wilkins have always been so close. I do hope this won't destroy their friendship," returned Mrs. Brown, whose husband helped run the mill.

Florence took a step closer to them.

"I'm sorry, but I couldn't help overhearing. I assure you Marcus Johnson is here. He was outside visiting with that Lieutenant Hawkins," she informed them.

"Oh, thank you, dear. Glad to hear it. I saw the lieutenant when we arrived. Seems to be a nice gentleman for a Yankee," responded Mrs. Tate.

Arnold arrived with apple cider and plates with pie. Mrs. Tate and Mrs. Brown excused themselves. Arnold led her to one of the benches that had been placed around the perimeter of the dance floor. Florence sat slowly, still unaccustomed to the new, heavier taffeta material of her dress. The cotton of her day dress was so much softer and lighter.

"Thank you, Mr. Beasley," she said.

It was so hard for her to remember to be formal with him.

"Of course, Miss Cushman. Now that we have a moment, I would like to pursue the question of an engagement. I have waited in order to give you time to get used to the idea. However, you surely realize it is inevitable. There are no other eligible young men of which your family would approve. These are difficult times. Tonight is not the appropriate time, but I do want it to be soon. Therefore, I am asking you for your hand in marriage now, but with the understanding that the announcement will have to be a later time."

He watched her face carefully.

"Arnold, I mean, Mr. Beasley, I appreciate your patience, but I'm afraid I must ask for an extension of that patience."

"There is no reason to persist in this resistance. We will be married," he stated in an impatient whisper and then quickly looked around to confirm no one had overheard.

He recoiled slightly as he encountered the unblinking, golden gaze of Boyd Richards, who had approached them without notice.

"Mr. Beasley, may I please have the pleasure of one dance with Miss Cushman. I promise to return her promptly."

Boyd's Georgian drawl was deep and smooth. His manner was completely Southern gentleman. Florence had forgotten his native state until that moment. She had not seen the man who had been brought up with plantation parties until now. He was very impressive. Arnold must have thought likewise, because he readily agreed. Boyd bowed slightly and offered her his hand.

Mr. Richards was, without question, the best dancer she had ever known; not that she had danced with so many. The farm boys she had danced with as a youth were fair. Her cousin, Ian, from Virginia, who had visited last year, was pretty good, but this was like floating. She became self-conscious and was afraid she would stumble, but the music and they continued, both flowing like the river. The man was strong and steady. His Nancy had been a lucky woman. Florence continued to stare at his shoulder. He was so tall she barely reached it, and she certainly couldn't see over it. She was startled when she heard his voice.

"Miss Cushman, thank you for a wonderful dance. It has been a long time, and I'm afraid I'm a little rusty."

"Not at all, Mr. Richards. You are a wonderful dancer." She tilted her head back in time to see a flicker of pain cross his face.

The music ended, and he looked down at her now anxious face. "Thank you. Now, I must return you to Mr. Beasley."

He reached for her arm to turn her in the right direction, but instead of taking her by the elbow, he reached for her upper arm and felt her wince. He turned his back, blocking Arnold's impatient stare. Without asking, he gently slid down her shawl. She had kept it hooked in the bends of her elbows so it stayed around her, covering her upper arms, just under the puffy short sleeves of her dress. She had known without looking that Arnold's grip earlier that evening had left bruises. She could feel them, and she knew Boyd saw the purple patches on her upper left arm. She pulled back and quickly reposi-tioned her shawl.

"Please, don't say anything. I upset him," she implored him.

Boyd's eyes were angry, but his face was a stone mask. "There is no excuse for this, Miss Cushman. He is no gentleman, he is no man, and he is just a boy, a selfish boy."

He saw her anxiously glance around him. He turned and escorted her back to Arnold, who was now standing, awaiting them.

"Thank you for allowing me the privilege of Miss Cushman's company," said Boyd. Then he turned and, in a quick flourish, bowed and was gone.

Florence watched him make his way to where Marcus was standing close to the musicians. Lieutenant Hawkins was also there. Florence thought that strange, but before she could ponder it a moment more, Arnold stepped in front of her, blocking her view.

"What did you and Mr. Richards stop to discuss after your dance?" Arnold demanded.

"Nothing of importance. We discussed dancing," she replied.

"Florence, I demand you tell—"

The voice of Mrs. Johnson asking for everyone's attention interrupted them. They, along with everyone present, turned their focus to the woman in the tan brocade dress who stood at the center of the room. Her smile encompassed everyone.

"I am sure everyone is having as wonderful a time as I am. Thank you, friends and neighbors, for being here. We will return to the music and dancing shortly, but it is now time to present the two men for which this night was planned: my son, Marcus Johnson, and his friend, John Wilkins."

There were shouts and clapping as Marcus and John joined Emily Johnson in the middle of the room. She hugged them both and then crossed to stand beside her husband. John and Marcus held their hands up to silence the clapping.

"We both are so humbled by this welcome home, especially since it took us so long to come home," said John.

This brought a somber silence. The pastor stepped forward. "That is over, boys. We are just glad you did come home."

Several supportive comments were shouted from the onlookers.

"Ma, thank you and all the people who worked for this evening. You are special. Now, speaking of special people, Mr. Alan Cushman has an announcement he would like to share. Mr. Cushman," stated Marc.

Florence watched John and Marcus step back as her father came forward. He looked so dignified and proud. "Friends, it is with great pride and pleasure I announce the engagement of my eldest daughter, Dawn, to John Wilkins. Dawn and John, please come here."

Florence watched as her beautiful sister, looking happier than could be imagined, was escorted to the place of honor beside their pa. There was tremendous applause. Then Florence turned as she felt Arnold move away from her. His father and Lieutenant Hawkins were whispering to him. Arnold looked up at her as they spoke and then crossed to her briefly.

"Florence, my pa and Lieutenant Hawkins need me to go with them for a little while. I am sure I will be able to return shortly. Excuse me," he said in a clipped manner and was gone.

Florence turned back to where her sister and John stood and tried to focus on their words.

"There have been many changes in all our lives. We have survived, and God has brought many blessings out of adversity. He surprised me with this lovely young woman I have known all my life. I am so thankful she has done me the honor of consenting to be my wife. Now, in answer to the question I have been asked many times since we returned, I plan to settle here and build a life with my bride after we are wed," declared John, looking completely at peace.

Everyone cheered, and he slowly bowed low and kissed Dawn's hand. She blushed prettily. John then held up his hand to quiet down the crowd once again.

"My future father-in-law has another announcement, Mr. Cushman."

Florence suddenly went cold as she saw her father walk to the place formerly occupied by Dawn and John. He looked grim. She knew that look. She had seen it many times when she had displeased him. Something was wrong.

"Friends, you also know my middle daughter, Florence. Florence, come here."

HOME ALWAYS BECKONS ~ 123

Florence looked around as eyes turned on her. She didn't have a choice. She slowly wove her way through to her pa. Once there, he put an arm around her, and she sucked in her breath as he unknowingly pressed against one of her bruised arms. She glanced up at him and saw him tense. He then removed his arm and took her hand.

"After this evening, you have probably surmised that Arnold Beasley is courting her."

Florence thought she would faint. *Surely, he wasn't! Where was Arnold? Please, Pa, don't announce our engagement. We are not engaged. I asked Arnold to wait,* she thought silently.

"Well, up to this point you would have been correct. However, I have been informed of a conflict in this area. His family has recently been in contact with a cousin who reminded them of prior arrangements with a family back east. Due to the war, these arrangements were questionable. It will be some time before a decision is made regarding these prior plans. Since there is another young man who is interested in my daughter's hand, I have decided to withdraw my approval of Arnold Beasley in favor of this other man."

Florence felt her heart race and her mouth grow dry. What was he talking about? Who was Arnold arranged to marry? More importantly, what other young man was interested in her? Her face was pale as she scanned the crowd. Her pa was now talking to her. She tried to focus.

"Florence, before I introduce this man, you must

know that he wants an immediate answer as to if you will have him. Of course, you will have a courtship period, but he needs to know that there will be a wedding to come."

She couldn't take it all in clearly, but a future with anyone besides Arnold, after the side she had seen of him tonight, seemed more promising. She would never have Matt back again, so she would trust her pa's judgment. Florence felt herself nodding.

"Very well, now, friends, it gives me pleasure to announce the engagement of my middle daughter, Florence Elizabeth Cushman, to Marcus Johnson. Marcus, please come here and join us."

Marcus! Everything seemed to move in slow motion. His tall, muscled but slender frame moved to stand beside her. Then he was looking down at her with serious emerald eyes. His tanned face looked almost menacing for a moment as he frowned, his mustached upper lip pressed in a grim manner as the muscle in his jaw twitched. His dark brown hair was pushed back from his forehead, and she suddenly had the impulse to pull it forward, like he used to wear it.

He saw the shock and concern on her face. How could he make it easier? It would take her some time to get used to the idea. It was going to take him a while to get used to this new development. The crowd clapped, but he could tell they were waiting for Florence to say something.

"This evening has been full of surprises. Please, give Florence a chance to adjust. I will. My childhood shadow has just agreed to marry me without knowing it was me. I would like to have the chance to dance with her right now."

A cheer and well wishes were shouted from their neighbors and friends. Then the music was playing, and Marcus was holding her as they waltzed across the floor. She felt the tension slowly seeping from her body. Little bits of the evening's events were replaying in her head. One of the things that kept replaying was something Marcus had said; she had to correct his misconception.

"Marcus ... Mr. Johnson."

"Florence, call me Marc."

"Marc, I wasn't your childhood shadow. I was Matt's. You need to know that."

"I know that. I've learned a lot since I came home. But we were still friends, right?" Marc asked in a gentle tone.

She nodded.

The music ended, and Marcus led her through the milling couples to the steps of the courthouse. The light from the party spilled onto the first step, and they sat. This was not an easy task with her full dress.

"Florey, please remove your shawl, and let me see what Arnold did to you."

As she slowly complied, everything began to fall in place.

"Mr. Richards told you, and you told my pa?"

His face was steel as he gently touched the bruised areas on both arms. He couldn't believe that Arnold would have dared to treat her so roughly. He saw her watching him with wide eyes.

"Actually, Lieutenant Hawkins overheard you and Arnold, as well as saw him grab you. He asked to speak with me to find out more about both of you. It really surprised me, a Yankee, who looks at things a lot like I do."

"But Marc, that didn't mean you had to ask for my hand."

"Oh, yes it did. When we told your ma and pa, they were both very upset. However, your ma kept saying, 'Who will marry her now?' and something about sending you to Virginia," he said, as if that explained everything.

"Marc, I am not your responsibility. I am eighteen years old. God will take care of me." Suddenly a tremor went through her, and she remembered her prayers over these past weeks. "He has taken care of me." She looked up at Marc in wonder and peace.

Marc's gaze locked with hers. "He has also taken care of me."

She shivered, and he wrapped her shawl around her.

"I better get you back."

He rose and helped her to her feet. She got off balance slightly, and he steadied her. She smiled at him awkwardly and turned to go. The moonlight cast a soft light on her face and upswept hair.

"Florence." He reached out for her hand.

She turned back to him, and he studied her face. He had seen it when he came home, but he hadn't dwelt on it until now. She would have caused him to take a second look if they had just met. The white ribbons that had been woven into her hair dangled delicately on the soft curve of her throat and shoulders. He reached his right hand up, slowly tracing the high cheekbones and the gentle slope of her jaw.

"I want to marry you."

She felt tears well up in her eyes. She reached up for his hand, which was touching her face. It was a strong hand, but it had a gentle touch. He would never use it to harm her, she knew it. She slowly turned his palm over and rested her face in it briefly before releasing it. Then she reached up and shyly pulled some of his hair forward on his forehead.

"I like it better that way," she said with a smile.

He grinned, and then the music drifted out and reached them.

"Florence, may I have this dance?"

"Yes, Marcus," she replied and moved into his arms.

The moonlight glowed as they danced under the star-filled sky. Ella and Alan Cushman had come to look for them but stopped as they saw the young couple. Alan had a lump in his throat. Richard had been astute in his judgment. His son had taken great satisfaction punching the young Mr. Beasley after they had escorted him from the dance. He shuddered to think of the years of misery that had surely faced his daughter had they not found out Arnold's true character. There really was a young lady back east, but her family had stopped considering the union due to the

Beasley's Confederate ties. However, the family had recently written to them to say they may have been too hasty. The Beasleys had not answered the letter yet, due to Arnold courting Florence. He wasn't sure what would happen with Arnold now. However, he did know that his daughter had been rescued due to the care of Marcus, Boyd, and Lieutenant Hawkins, and more importantly, the good Lord above.

He had always hoped Marcus Johnson would be his son-in-law.

Chapter
Six

Florence awoke with a start and sat straight up in bed. She was engaged to Marcus Johnson! It all seemed surreal. She felt someone watching her and looked over to where Dawn lay smiling sleepily.

"Good morning, sister. Can you believe it? I am so happy for you, as well as myself. I'm sorry that I didn't tell you about John and me."

Florence pushed her pillow against the wooden headboard, pulled her knees up, and looked down at her sister.

"I understand, but now I want to know how it all happened. The last thing I had concluded was that you were interested in Mr. Richards."

Dawn nodded and sat up beside Florence.

"It started out that way. I tried to visit with him when I brought their lunches but found myself talking to John more and more instead. He has become a wonderful man who loves the Lord and has been able to take everything he has been through and put it to work to help others. John and I have really been talking with Boyd. Boyd is a good man, but he does not have a relationship with the Lord. He is so full of bitterness and regret. The Lord is the only way he will be able to truly move on. Please pray for him."

"I will. I have been. You know, he asked me to dance last night. I think Marcus wanted him to check on me because Lieutenant Hawkins had reported to him," said Florence.

She slowly pushed up the right sleeve of her gown, revealing the now deep purple and reddish bruises. Dawn gasped and took her sister's left arm, rolling up that sleeve. There was one lid-sized bruise there also. They were both staring at it when their ma entered the room. Florence started to roll her sleeves down, but her ma sat down on the edge of the bed and stilled her hand's activity.

"Let me look, Florence," said her ma. "Dawn, go take a rag and dip it in the cold well water I just sat by the door. Wait; bring two for your sister."

Dawn quickly disappeared through the door.

"Florence, I am sorry this happened. I would have never thought Arnold capable of this." Her mother's eyes met hers.

Florence could tell her mother was feeling guilty and quickly said, "No one could have known. I mean, I knew he wanted to control me, but even I never expected the anger he showed last evening."

"What upset him so?"

Florence dipped her head and answered without looking at her mother. "I told him about the picture of Matt."

She heard her mother suck in her breath and looked up to see a look of complete mortification.

"Oh, my dear one, truth has always strengthened your father's and my relationship. I was only thinking that would be true of Arnold. Please." She waited until Florence was looking directly at her. "Forgive me."

Her mother had never made that request of her in eighteen years. It touched her, and she reached for her mother's hand.

"Yes, ma'am. I love you."

Tears sprang into her mother's eyes, and then she blinked them away as Dawn entered the room with the cold cloths.

Florence lay down, and her mother gently placed the rags on both of her arms. Alice had awakened and padded over to her older sister's bed. She sat on the foot of the bed, yawning sleepily. Her eyes widened slightly at the sight of her sister's injuries. Will had finally sought out his parents to explain things after all the announcements the previous evening. Alice had been full of so many questions that his ears had been hurting.

"I bet Marcus wanted to beat up Arnold about this," stated Alice firmly.

"Alice, he did no such a thing. I believe Marcus has seen enough violence in his lifetime," Ella reprimanded her youngest child.

"Well, at least Marcus is marrying her and not Arnold. You never really liked Arnold anyway, did you, Florence?" Alice continued.

"Alice!" Her ma's tone warned her to halt.

"It's all right, Ma." Florence smiled at her younger sister and whispered, "No, I did not."

Alice smiled in return, quite satisfied. Their mother frowned at them and looked to Dawn for support but caught her smiling as well. She threw up her hands in exasperation and stood up to leave.

"Florence, you stay here until the rags become warm, and then you girls are to dress and do your chores. Don't forget, you are to help Jenny today. The doc says it could be any day now."

She gave her daughters a last firm look before leaving the room. She heard their laughter as she shut the door, and she smiled.

The early morning found Marcus walking toward the Wilkins' farm. He had awakened in the wee hours before dawn with this thought. The dreams and flashes from the past that disturbed his sleep had seemed even more real. He hoped he could make it to his destination without being discovered. The back fields were dew-covered, moistening his boots as the tree that stood about thirty feet from the back of the Wilkins' house came into view. His steps slowed as he saw the cross that was placed in the shade of the old tree's branches. Matt's body wasn't here; it lay with those of his fellow fallen comrades from the battle at Chickamauga, Georgia. There had only been one local soldier buried on the actual battlefield, but the rest had been moved for burial, most still far from home. However, Mrs. Wilkins had asked her husband to place this cross in his memory. He had found John here, quietly remembering his little brother, last week when he had come over at Boyd's request to talk about a letter he had received from Texas.

Now Marc removed his hat and moved to stand in front of the memorial marker. He looked up, staring at the strong, sheltering branches and then back down at the ground.

"Lord, I know the earthly body of Matt's is not here, and besides that, he is with you anyway, but I have some things I need to say to him. I pray you will please help me get these words to him." He paused, exhaled a deep breath, then began, "Matt, I—," he felt his throat constrict, and his Adam's apple bobbed up and down as he swallowed hard, "I've got something to tell you and hope it is something you favor. But first, I just want you to know how much I have come to admire who you were. It's funny, in a sad sort of way, how we never seem to see people as clearly until we look back at them. To think, you wanted to be like me. It's only now that I realize it's me who should have tried to be more like you. You really studied people. Things I had not focused on at the time they were happening have come flooding back so clearly. Last night I remembered you helping that boy from south Texas write a letter home, since he couldn't write. The way you fought, so bravely, even being as young as you were. Then the way Richard told us about your concern for those you loved as you died. Well, boy, I wish you could be here with us

HOME ALWAYS BECKONS ~ 135

now." Marc stopped awkwardly, trying to find how to say it. "Matt, I spoke to Richard and John about what I'm fixing to tell you, and you probably already know. Florence and I are to be married. It happened so fast…I just knew I couldn't let Arnold have her. I promise to be good to her. Anyway, I just wanted you to know."

The silence of the morning surrounded him, and his voice sounded strange to his ears. He looked around, replaced his hat, and turned, retracing his steps toward his parents' home.

John Wilkins watched his friend's retreating figure from the back window and turned at the sound of his mother's footsteps. She quietly came to stand beside him and shared his view. As Marcus disappeared from sight, she turned, nodded, and patted his shoulder before going to start breakfast.

"It's the right thing. He's a good man," was all she said.

❧

Florence had been helping Jenny all morning. They were talking about the events of the previous night as they were setting lunch on the table when Jenny doubled over. Florence set down the plate she was holding and rushed over to her sister-in-law.

"Jenny, is it the baby?" she asked.

Jenny straightened. "Yes, I've been feeling small pains all morning. I just didn't want to say anything until I was sure. Help me to the bedroom."

Florence quickly completed the request and helped Jenny into bed.

Jenny grabbed her hand as Florence straightened the covers. "Go get Richard, and then go get Doc."

Florence nodded. "I'll be quick."

Richard had gone to the mill. Florence met him returning halfway there. He saw her face and turned white and swallowed hard. He dropped the sack he was carrying and started running, stopped, and came back and picked up the sack and frowned at Florence, who was still standing there.

"Florence, don't just stand there. Go get Doc, and then go get Ma."

Brother and sister took off in opposite directions, both moving as fast as their feet would carry them and heedless of the many stares of the townspeople.

Mr. and Mrs. O'Neal paused from their activities at their store's entrance and watched the Cushman siblings. They exchanged glances and smiled.

"I do believe Jenny's time is at hand, Clyde." Mr. O'Neal smiled at his wife.

"I feel she will do fine. I'm not so sure about Richard."

She patted his hand. "You survived it five times, dear."

He chuckled. "Yes, but the first was the real test."

They both laughed and returned to their work.

Florence found Doc at his office and then quickly headed for home. She found Ma and Dawn baking inside.

"Dawn, you stay here and finish the baking. It probably will be a while. After you finish, bring Alice and come to Richard's," Ella said and then turned to Florence, who was still trying to catch her breath. "Florence, your pa is over at the Johnson's helping Lee and the boys with that hog pen. Run over there and tell him. He can come when he's ready."

Florence took a deep breath. "Yes, ma'am."

The baby will be here before I reach everybody, she thought as she ran down the porch steps.

Marcus saw Florence at a distance and started forward. He was alarmed to see her running so hard. However, Alan Cushman had also seen his approaching daughter and reached her before Marcus.

Alan grabbed his daughter and steadied her. "Florence, what's happened?" he asked in a firm tone.

Florence gasped two breaths before she was able to answer. "Jenny … baby's coming … Ma said come when you can."

Alan looked relieved. Will hurried to Florence with a dipper of water, which she gulped gratefully. Alan waited until she finished.

"Florence, you shouldn't have run that way. I thought something bad had happened. Jenny's strong, and if your ma and Doc are there, it will be fine. I'll go directly. We are almost finished here."

Florence couldn't believe he was so calm. Richard sure hadn't been. After she had run all over the place, bringing the news, he was not in a rush to go. She turned to hide the perplexed look she felt forming on her face. However, Marc saw it and had to hide a smile. He did not want her mad at him the first day of their engagement.

"Mr. Cushman, allow me to take Florence in to get some refreshment from Ma. She can rest a bit and wait for us to finish before returning to town," he said and saw Florence quickly turn to look at him.

"That's a fine idea, Marcus. Florence, go inside, and I'll come get you when I'm ready to go," said Alan, and then he walked away with Lee Johnson.

Florence caught her breath and straightened her shoulders, suddenly conscious of how disheveled she must look. Marc was staring at her steadily, and it made her nervous.

"I think I should go back to town. Jenny might need me," she said and then self-consciously licked her dry lips.

Marc slowly walked to stand directly in front of her.

"You heard your pa. Besides, I think Jenny has plenty of help right now," he said with a slight smile.

He saw her glance in the direction of the hog pen where her pa stood. "Florey, you have to remember, your pa has been through this a few times with your ma."

She looked back to encounter his tolerant gaze. "I know, but not with a daughter-in-law and a son. Don't you think he should be in a bit more of a hurry to get there?"

He lifted one eyebrow. "I have no idea, Florence.

I don't have any children at this point." He saw her blush as the implication for their future hit her, and he couldn't resist. "Maybe we will both know more about it in a few years. We can talk about it then."

She looked around, up, down, anywhere but at him. What was she supposed to say to that? This was so strange, Marcus and her. It would take time to adjust. She felt his hand take her by the elbow, and she glanced at him out of the corner of her eye as he led her to the house. He looked straight ahead until they reached the door, and he looked down at her.

"Florence, go visit with Ma and relax. Your pa and I will come and get you directly."

She nodded, and then he strode across the yard to join in the work that was being completed.

Mrs. Johnson looked up from her churning as Florence came through the door. She could see the slight apprehension on the young woman's face. This was to be her daughter-in-law, and she wanted their relationship to be close. The girl had now closed the door and was standing there stiffly.

"I'm sorry to intrude, but Marcus said I should wait here. You see, Jenny's baby is coming, and Ma sent me to tell Pa, and Pa wants to finish the work out there first." She gestured toward the door and thought how silly she sounded. Her skin flushed crimson.

Emily glanced downward to hide the smile that played about her mouth. She rose and walked quickly toward Florence. Her hands were outstretched in welcome.

"Florence, this is such a treat. I was hoping we would find some time to talk. Please come in and sit with me."

They shared a smile, and Florence reached out to take the outstretched hands. Emily ushered the young woman to a chair across from the one behind the churn.

"May I finish that for you?" Florence offered, looking at the churn.

Emily Johnson looked surprised and then pleased. However, she shook her head as she resumed her seat and began manipulating the dasher.

"Thank you, dear, but I'm almost finished. We can pour the butter molds in a bit. Talking to you will make the chore pass faster. Mary Wilkins has talked of you so fondly through the years. You must be very special. I thought she was just influenced by the fact that her youngest son loved you, but now ... you've captured my son's heart as well," she returned.

Florence shook her head. "Oh, I don't know about that," then she quickly added, "begging your pardon, ma'am." She bit her lip as if silently reprimanding herself.

One of Emily's eyebrows shot up in an expression reminiscent of Marcus. The dasher kept moving steadily.

"Florence, what part don't you know about?" the older woman challenged.

"Well, the special part for sure. Just ask my parents how difficult I am. The other part, about capturing Marcus's heart, I mean, I know we are to be married, but it's not like that." Her gray eyes anxiously scanned the face opposite her. She took in the blue-green eyes, which narrowed thoughtfully.

Suddenly the dasher stilled and Emily removed the lid.

"Florence, let us take care of the butter, and then we will have a long talk."

Florence swallowed hard. "Yes, ma'am," she said as she rose to assist.

It was about an hour later when they resumed their seats, both with a glass of cool water in hand. Emily moved her chair beside Florence's and then scooted to the edge of her seat before turning to take Florence's hands in hers.

"Florence Cushman, I want you to look at me and listen carefully. You are special. God made you, and his son died for you. That above all else makes you special. Now, as for being difficult, the tales of your less-than-lady-like childhood escapades are well known throughout our town. But you are by no means the only little girl who did not like ribbons, frill, and indoor chores. I just hope you've learned enough to keep my son from eating raw meat and wearing dirty clothes. You have, haven't you?" She saw the blush, heard the slightly nervous laugh, and saw the nod of affirmation before continuing. "Good. Now, in regard to my son's feelings for you, I know he has always been fond of you. I also know that my son would not have assured that you would be his wife unless he found you special. No, I have not questioned the depth of his feelings for you. He is grown and has also known you long enough to make that decision. These things say to me that you have captured his heart. Has he captured yours?"

Emily had tried to speak with kindness and candor in order to ease the knots she knew must be in Florence's stomach. She smiled as Florence took a deep breath and answered with obvious honesty.

"Marcus always had my admiration as a child. It dimmed a bit when he didn't come home and I saw the hurt it caused your family and my brother, Richard. Yet when he came home, I saw something in his eyes that first day. I can't explain it. I could understand somehow. Then I thought he would be Dawn's beau. There was Arnold, who did not capture anything but my irritation." She smiled and found Emily smiling back with understanding. "Then there was Matt." She grew serious and her voice lowered. "I loved him always. I was still a girl when he left and he not much more than a boy. We did not have the chance to see what would have been. God had other plans. Mrs. Johnson, you must know this, Marcus was an answer to prayer." She explained her dilemma and prayers regarding her relationship with Arnold and the events of the party. When she finished, she looked down at her hands, which were in her lap, and then looked up. "I will try to be a good wife to Marcus. I like him, admire, and respect him. I wish I could say more."

Emily initially had wanted the girl to say she loved Marcus. She and Alan had loved each other when they married. However, as Florence had spoken, Emily found she really appreciated the girl's

HOME ALWAYS BECKONS ~ 143

honesty, and the girl did care for her son. She suspected both Marc and Florence probably cared more than either realized. Her mind searched for a way she could help and support them. Memories of her father and mother talking to Alan and her as they began their courtship washed over her. That was it! She would speak with Alan, and then they would talk to Marc and Florence. The manner in which her parents had structured their courtship had given them such a strong friendship, mutual respect, keen awareness of each other, and a deep love for each other. She knew there were obvious differences, but all the ingredients were there.

The door opened, interrupting her thoughts, and Marcus entered.

"Florey, your pa is ready to go. If you don't mind, I thought I would go with you. Richard and Jenny's baby will be my niece or nephew once we are married. I'd like to be there."

He looked so boyish standing there with his hat in his hand, both women felt tender toward him.

"Of course, I don't mind. That's so nice of you." Florence stood and turned to Mrs. Johnson. "Thank you so much for your kindness. I enjoyed our talk."

Emily rose.

"As did I, dear," she said then turned and crossed to her son. "Marcus, you're pa and I would like to visit with you and Florence together. We will speak with the Cushmans and then plan on visiting perhaps tomorrow night. Maybe your brothers can visit with the Cushmans at that time. Now, you two run along. Please give my best to Richard and Jenny."

Marcus looked slightly worried.

He smiled, "Yes, Ma. Florey, let's go."

Emily smiled in parting as her future daughter-in-law turned to walk through the doorway where Marcus stood holding the door open.

Florence continued across the porch and down the front step, stopping where her pa sat waiting on his horse. She was reaching up for her pa to give her a hand up so she could ride behind him when she felt two hands around her waist.

"Florence, why don't you ride with me," Marcus said, turning her toward him, half in question and half making a statement.

She turned toward her pa. The look of paternal protection was soon veiled as he met Marc's solid gaze. He nodded to Florey. Marc gathered his horse's reins and swung easily into the saddle. Florence put a foot in the stirrup he had left open for her, reached for the down-stretched arm, and was pulled up to settle behind Marc. They turned their horses, waved to Mr. Johnson and the boys, and headed toward town.

Florence had often ridden behind her father and brother, even Matt, and she had never been uncomfortable. Now she felt like she couldn't breathe and even in the very cool autumn evening felt overly warm. They did not speak the entire way to town.

She felt like she would scream or faint before they reached Richard's house.

Finally, they reached the small farm house and Florence quickly dismounted, not waiting for Marc to help her. She knew both her pa and Marc had noticed, but she did not care at this point. It felt like a matter of survival. She had to breathe, and she was not doing very well with Marc so close. It was the strangest thing, and she did not like it one bit.

She burst through the door to find Richard pacing. The bedroom door was closed, and there were soft and then loud moans coming from the other side. Alice sat in front of the fireplace, biting her fingernails with very wide eyes. Dawn and John sat awkwardly at the table, quietly talking to each other. Florence saw Marc freeze as he entered the room and heard the sounds of pain. Her pa calmly walked over to Richard and clasped him on the shoulder.

"Son, you had might as well try to relax. The first one takes the longest," he assured his son in a matter-of-fact tone.

Richard looked his father in the eye and found assurance there.

"Thanks, Pa." He exhaled loudly. "I was beginning to imagine the worst. I was in there at first, and then when the doctor and Ma got here, it got too crowded. I wasn't helping."

Alan Cushman got a knowing look on his face, and then a thought occurred to him. One of his most special memories was of Alice's birth, because he had actually been in the room when she came into the world. He had been sent out during the births of his other children. He cocked his head to the side and contemplated everyone's reaction to what he was about to do. He grabbed Richard by the arm and ushered him toward the closed door.

"Pa, what are you doing?" Richard asked uncertainly.

"Son, I was only allowed to watch the actual birth of Alice. It is an experience you should not miss. You will appreciate Jenny even more if you are with her during this time. Your mother has been in there long enough. It is your turn," Alan said.

Richard gave him a look that said he hoped his pa planned to inform his mother. Alan nodded and opened the door. Ella Cushman and the doctor looked shocked at the interruption. Alan quickly crossed to his wife and whispered in her ear, causing the protests that were forming on her lips to go unspoken. A gentle look passed between them. She turned and bent over the bed, taking Jenny's hand.

"It's Richard's time to be with you now. I'll be outside if you need me," she whispered to her daughter-in-law, who was between labor pains.

Jenny nodded, her eyes finding Richard's as another pain gripped her, causing her to shut her eyes and gasp, her body consumed with the pangs of giving birth. He moved quickly to her side, swallowing hard. He had witnessed many things, but seeing his wife in pain was the worst thing at that moment.

His parents quietly left the room. Jenny's knees were bent, and the doctor checked her progress again. He looked at Richard. It was time for Jenny to start pushing. He hoped the young man was ready to watch his child being born. It had been his experience that men who had helped in the births of numerous livestock still found human birth hard to witness.

"Jenny, I want you to push when I tell you it's time. Your little one is ready. I can see his or her head," said Doc.

Jenny propped up on her elbows, Richard beside her, supporting her back, and the first series of pushing cycles began.

Then suddenly a little body emerged into Doc's hands. He turned the tiny body around, announcing, "You have a son!"

A loud cry filled the room.

Richard knew he had never shared a more wonderful experience, and Jenny could not remember a single pain of labor. The umbilical cord was cut, and young David Matthew Cushman was laid on his mother's chest—David for Jenny's father and Matthew for Matt Wilkins, their friend. Richard kissed his wife gently and tentatively touched the face of his new son. The doctor finished the afterbirth procedures with Jenny and then opened the door to ask Ella to come back in to help clean up her new grandson.

Ella entered, smiling broadly at the small family on the bed. Richard gave Jenny another kiss before excusing himself. Ella gently reached for her new grandson and took him to the table covered with blankets. She took the warm rags the doctor handed

148 ~ LANA LYNNE

her and cleansed his newborn body as the doctor gently examined him. He was then wrapped in a warm blanket. The doctor held him as Ella covered Jenny with fresh blankets, propped her up on pillows, then young David was placed in his mother's waiting arms.

The waiting family and soon to be family members were then allowed to go in by twos to visit briefly with mother and child. Florence and Marc stood in the doorway as John and Dawn stood beside the bed gazing down at Jenny and her new son. There was moisture reflected in John's eyes as his lingering gaze left the infant and found Richard.

"David Matthew Cushman. It is a fine name, Richard. Matt would be very proud of his namesake. Thank you." John turned to address Jenny. "And thank you for that honor, Jenny. He is a fine boy."

"We are honored to remember the fine young man your brother was. I pray our little David Matthew will grow up to be like him," Jenny returned seriously.

John turned away as Dawn bent to gently hug her sister-in-law and new nephew. He found Florence's watery gaze on him and walked over to enfold her in a hug. No words were spoken. John let go and then quickly exited the room. It was then that Florence noticed the almost statue-like state of her fiancée. Marc's face was a stony mask, and his jaw was clenched. As he noticed her observation, he abruptly left the room. He was already out the door and the sound of hoof beats signaled his departure before Florence reached the front porch.

"Marcus!" she called.

"Florence, let him go," said John from behind her.

"But why did he leave like that?" she asked with a quizzical and perplexed look on her face. She leaned her head against the porch pole closest to her, wrapping an arm around it as if to find comfort.

John smiled slightly at her innocence. "Well, little one, he is finding it hard to compete with the memory of my brother."

Her head shot up. "What? Oh!"

She whirled, facing the direction where Marc had galloped away. Then she quickly turned back to John. John swallowed hard. He knew that look. He had seen Florence become softer and quieter in the last couple of weeks. He should have known it couldn't last. The determined young woman before him still had what had made Matt so admire her. His brother loved her feistiness. It was such a contrast to his reserved nature; he said he always felt so alive when he was with her. John was now a little fearful for Marcus. It was almost impossible to stop Florence in this mood.

"Florey, what are you planning?" John spoke quietly as if to a skittish colt.

"John, please tell Pa I'll meet them at home. I'm going to see Marcus."

Her eyes flashed, and she was down the steps and on her Pa's horse before John could speak.

"Florence Cushman, it's not right for you to go over there like this," he called to a stir of dust. He shook his head and headed for the door.

Dawn came out, saw his face, and noticed her pa's missing horse.

"Florey's done it again. Just when Pa and Ma were starting to relax a bit," she said in resignation. Then with a spark in her eye, "Will you tell Pa? Please?"

Those blue eyes were his undoing, and he smiled, taking her hand. "For you? Anything."

They turned as her pa came out the door.

"What's going on? I hear a horse riding away and shouting. A baby and his mother are trying to fall asleep. Wait. Where's my horse?"

"Florence," they said in unison.

That was all Alan needed to hear. He would find out the details later. He would also have a talk with Marcus Johnson. If the man was going to be his son-in-law, he better learn to handle his daughter.

∾

Florence reached the Johnson farm and saw the lantern was still lit in the barn. She quickly dismounted and hurried into the barn to find Marcus brushing down his mustang. A thunder cloud appeared to be over his head. He barely glanced up, much less looked in the least surprised to see her.

"Go home, Florence," was all he said as he continued his firm brush strokes across the shiny dark coat.

The animal shifted and whinnied in protest at

the new arrival. He finished his chore and then went to fill the feed trough in the stall. That finished, he closed the gate across the stall, picked up the lantern, and started out the barn door. Florence did not move.

He turned as he stated, "Unless you want to spend the night in there, I suggest you come out now. I'd like to close the door and go in the house."

She took that as an invitation and walked past him and then waited for him as he bolted the door. He finished and then stopped in front of her.

"Go home, Florence. You should not be here. Do not make me any more angry than I already am," he bit out.

In the spill of light from the lantern, he saw her eyes flash. She looked like a defiant little girl.

He sighed wearily. "Florence, you don't even know why I'm mad. You're just mad because I'm mad at you and you don't know why, right?"

He saw her shoulders, which were squared for battle, give a bit.

"In a way, Marc, I know it has something to do with Matt. John said it is because it is hard for you to compete with Matt's memory. Please explain. I have agreed to be your wife. There is no competition," her voice stated firmly and then became soft.

Marc saw the troubled gray eyes searching his face for an answer. The difference in their ages and experiences was suddenly glaringly apparent. It was not her fault, and he owed it to her to try and explain.

152 ~ LANA LYNNE

He took a step closer to her and gazed down at her upturned face.

"Florey, I'm mad at myself, I'm mad at you, and I'm mad at Matt. At me, because I'm mad at Matt. He was the nicest kid. He should be here with you. I'm mad at you because of all the things you still feel for him." He put his hand up as she started to speak. Then he crossed to the corral and propped on the top rail, gazing at the stars. "I know God spared me. I know he forgave me when I ran from him and my family after the war. Florence, I quit caring for a while. The men Boyd, John, and I worked cattle with were rough. So were we. I've done a lot of things I'm not proud of, and if you knew, well, you would not have agreed to marry me."

He spoke with his back toward her, so she couldn't see his face, but she could hear the remorse in his voice. She moved beside him, noticing how he dwarfed her in height, the finely chiseled jaw line, and the large hands, which were now gripping the top rail of the corral fence. The changes the years had made in him suddenly washed over her.

She spoke quietly. "Marcus, in many ways you are a different person from the one I grew up with. I would like to get to know you as you are now..." She paused and let her eyes linger on the muscle that was twitching in his jaw. "To hear about the man you were in between the war and now."

He turned slowly to face her with one hand on the railing. His eyes leisurely explored her face, taking in the tendrils the wind stirred at her hairline, the delicate curve of her neck, and the soft shape of her small mouth. Florence trembled. No one had ever looked at her like that. A masculine finger reached out to stroke the high slope of her left cheek, and she felt a tremor run through her. Marc felt it too and dropped his hand, starting to remove his coat.

Florence placed a stilling hand on his. "I'm not cold, Marcus."

He had to be sure of what she was saying. "Florence, I will never be Matt. I want us to remember him well, but I don't want to see him in your eyes whenever you get mad at me or I disappoint you. I know you are not in love with me, but I will care for you and protect you well."

Florence put a finger on his lips to halt his words and then hastily dropped her hand, blushing in the darkness. She turned back toward the corral. "Marc, this is so new. I mean us, engaged. I have always cared about you and … oh, can't we just give it time? Please, forgive me for keeping Matt so near in my words and thoughts. He was a part of both our lives. I will never forget him, but I want what you have so generously offered me."

He knew she was searching for words and then knew they didn't need any right now. Proper or not, he was going to kiss her. He didn't think she had ever been kissed, and even if she had, they had never kissed. His hand reached out for her shoulder, she turned, and his hand moved to cup her face. He briefly saw her eyes widen and then flutter shut as he angled his face over hers.

His lips were warm and firm and moved linger-
ingly over her mouth. She couldn't breathe again.
Then she felt her own lips move tentatively under
his. He lifted his head and her eyelids slowly opened
to find him watching her with a gentle light in his
eyes.

Before either one of them could speak, they heard
Lee Johnson's voice from the porch. "Son, I think
you two better come in the house. My friend, Alan,
would not take kindly to the fact that I have left you
without a chaperone. Besides, your ma and I want to
talk to you."

"But Pa, Ma said that would be tomorrow night,"
returned Marc.

"Now is better, I'm thinking," his pa said firmly.

"Yes, sir," he said.

Marc picked up the lantern with one hand and
took Florence by the elbow with the other one. They
quickly crossed to the house, both feeling like children being reprimanded.

Chapter

Seven

Boyd stared at John incredulously; he could not believe what he was hearing. John grinned as he removed his Sunday shirt and reached for one of his well-worn everyday shirts. His reaction had been the same when Marc told him after church.

Boyd shook his head. "Marc's parents want him to call on Florence every day, morning and evening, for three days in a row, and they can't speak to each other?"

John nodded. "It's something about them learning about each other without words or touch. They said that if Marc and Florey can become aware of and comfortable with each other like that, it will help them to appreciate each other more." He chuckled. "I know Marc can do it. We've all had to go long stretches without talking, but Florence ..."

Boyd remembered Florence's spirited tirade by the river and laughed. "Maybe his pa knows it's the only time of peace Marc will get!"

The two men started laughing so hard that Mr.

Wilkins came to the door to see what was happening, and then he began to laugh. Mary Wilkins was soon drawn by the sound and found them red faced with tears of mirth running down their cheeks. They tried to explain and then found that she did not find it funny at all. They simultaneously coughed, straightened, and headed for the outside. However, as soon as they reached the middle of the yard, the laughter started again. All Mary could do was to stand at the window watching them, shaking her head.

Florence sat by the fireplace, holding her nephew. Her mind was on Marcus. Their families had sat together in church, but they had been placed on opposite ends of the pew. She would not be seeing him again until tomorrow morning. He was to come and help her with her chores. Then he was supposed to come to call after supper. Tuesday morning she was to go and help him with his chores, stay and help his ma throughout the day, and then he was to walk her home before supper. Then Wednesday they were to go on a picnic during the middle of the day, and last they were to go to town and help Jenny and Richard. All activities were to be done without talking our touching. She lifted her right hand from where it rested on the blanketed infant, touching her lips briefly, recalling the kiss. Young David shifted against her left arm, and she quickly checked him. His little face was so sweet. He was starting to fuss, so she stood up and went to the bedroom where Jenny was resting.

Jenny stirred as she entered the room. She smiled as Florence laid the squirming bundle beside her.

"I think your son is ready for his lunch," said Florence. She turned to leave mother and son to their task, but was halted.

"Florey, please stay. I want to visit with you. Dawn is having lunch at the Wilkins', and your mother tells me your courtship is continuing also." She paused, watching the uncertain look pass over her sister-in-law's face. "She told me of the idea of the Johnsons' when you arrived after church. How do you feel about it?"

Florence bit her lip and then sat down on the foot of the bed. "I don't know. I'm a little afraid that he will realize how much I lack. I'm not pretty like Dawn."

Jenny was surprised. She never would have thought that Florence was insecure about her physical appearance. One of the reasons Jenny so admired Florey was her seeming ability to be as comfortable in a muddy dress as in a Sunday dress. Many of the young ladies of the county had had a hard time since the war, due not only to the destitute conditions, but especially the lack of new dresses to which they had been accustomed. Florence had not been concerned about this as a child or as she had grown, much to Mrs. Cushman's dismay at times. She had reminded Jenny of her own mother. The Indians had emphasized the inner person. But most surprising of all was the fact that Florence did not realize what a beautiful young woman she was. She turned her head toward the small dresser beside her bed.

"Florey, give me my hand mirror, please," she requested.

After Florence was repositioned at the foot of the bed, Jenny turned the mirror toward her. "Take a good look at your reflection."

Florey hesitated and then took the mirror and did Jenny's bidding. She frowned and laid down the mirror.

"No, Florey, I mean really look. See the wonderful changes that are taking place."

Florence looked, blushed, and then quickly replaced the mirror on the dresser. Jenny adjusted young David, who was still nursing, and covered Florey's hand with her own. Florence looked at her uncertainly.

"Florey, God has made you very lovely both inside and outside. Don't you see what Mr. and Mrs. Johnson want for you both? They want you to go beyond your words, beyond your outward appearances, and learn each other's specialness, which goes beyond those things. Think about your quiet times at your special spot. You become aware of nature; you appreciate the breeze, the changes of the seasons, and learn to listen to God. Do not be self-conscious. Become more conscious of Marc during these coming days and not yourself. Let him become more conscious of you and not of himself."

Both were quiet, and then David smacked and whimpered. They shared a smile and Florence rose.

"I'll take him and you can rest," Florence said, tenderly scooping up her nephew. She smiled at Jenny. "Thank you. I am so glad you are my sister-in-law."

She crossed to the door and closed it behind her. Her ma had just finished with the dishes and came to get her grandson.

"Where's Richard?' Florey asked.

Her ma inclined her head toward the door as she replied, "On the front porch with your pa and Alice."

"I'll be out there if you need me, Ma."

Florence found Alice sitting on the porch looking very bored as she listened to her brother and father discussing the continuing financial and government problems in the South.

"Pa, since we lost, I wish Lincoln had lived. That April 1865 was doom for the South; not just Lee's surrender, but when Booth shot President Lincoln, it surely adversely influenced the way this Reconstruction is being handled," Richard said.

"Now, Son, wait a minute. They say Andrew Johnson is trying to do things the way Lincoln would have," his pa countered.

Richard was shaking his head. "But he is not Lincoln. The men I know who met Lincoln and the things I've read—" He stopped as he noticed Florence and changed topics mid-sentence. "Is Jenny awake? Where's David?" He started to stand, but Florence

HOME ALWAYS BECKONS ~ 161

waved him down with her hands as she crossed to sit in the chair beside Alice.

"Jenny just nursed David and is now resting. Ma has David. Relax, young papa," she said with a smile.

Richard resumed his seat and was just about to resume his conversation with his father when young Alice's loud voice prevented it.

"Florence, I think this silent courting thing is the most ignorant thing I've ever heard. You won't marry Marc when you get through," Alice said with the utmost disdain and assurance.

Florence tried to hide a smile. "Why won't I marry him?"

Alice looked at her and rolled her eyes in exasperation. "Florey, when boys aren't talking or working, all they do is pick their noses, spit, and other boy things like that. Marc won't be able to help himself."

Richard burst out laughing, and their pa was trying to look stern as he said, "Alice, I don't think your mother would approve of such—," he said as his shoulders shook, and then he coughed, "talk."

Florence shot her brother a look to stop his laughter and turned to face her little sister with a somewhat straight face. "Alice, thank you for your thoughts. However, I think Marcus will try hard to refrain from such boyish things." *I hope,* she thought silently.

The sure, blue eyes of her little sister looked back

at her filled with certainty that Marc would surely disgrace himself.

A cold wind blew across the porch, and suddenly Florence was very cold. She saw Alice shiver, and then they both rose and turned toward the door.

Richard inclined his head. "Are you girls cold or something?" He grinned.

Alice put her hands on her hips. "Richard, it is almost Thanksgiving. It is usually getting colder by this time of year."

"Speaking of Thanksgiving," their pa interjected, "has your ma mentioned that we would like everyone, the Wilkins, the Johnsons, and our family, to have Thanksgiving at our house this year?"

"Yes, she mentioned it to Jenny. I think it will be a very special time," Richard said.

"No, we haven't talked about it. I guess I'll have to wait at least three days before I can talk to Marc about it," Florence said ruefully.

Alice put an arm around Florence's waist and gave her an affectionate squeeze.

"Don't worry about it. I'll tell him when he comes by tomorrow," she said and smiled impishly. "I still am allowed to talk to him."

Then she quickly ducked inside, barely missing the swat Florence directed at her backside. Florence shook her head and followed her sister inside. She knew it was time for them to be headed home, and ma would want help.

It was still dark outside, stars twinkling, as Marcus made his way to the Cushmans' farm. He could see his breath in the cold morning air and rubbed his hands together before thrusting them into his coat's pockets. He was nervous. It was one thing to go a day not talking with your friends. They were men, and battle, work, or hunting did not involve a lot of verbal communication. Women were different. It seemed like they were always talking. He was willing to bet that Florence was dreading the next three days. He had felt hopeful for an instant after their first kiss. His parents acknowledged he was a grown man, but at the same time, they had never asked anything of him since he had been home. It was the least he could do to show them respect. He just hoped he and Florence could survive it. As spirited as she was, she might decide to change her mind and run.

He stopped in front of their house and stood in the yard looking at the porch steps a minute before quietly mounting them. There weren't any flickers of light from the windows. He sat on one of the wooden chairs that were propped against the outer wall then pulled out his pocket watch and flipped it open. It read 4:00 a.m. They should be up within the hour. He leaned his head back against the wall and shut his eyes.

It was close to half an hour later when he heard footsteps inside and then the creak of the front door opening. He opened his eyes and turned his head, expecting Alan Cushman. His greeting stayed in his throat as he saw it was a still sleepy Florence shuffling out the door. The shadows covered him, and she did not turn her head. She was dressed, but her hair still spilled down her back, and she had forgotten her coat. He saw a shiver pass through her and started to rise, but she was moving down the steps and into the yard. He then realized that she was headed for the outhouse and knew she would be embarrassed if she saw him.

He smiled; she looked so tousled and sleepy. It reminded him of the time he, Richard, and John had taken Matt fishing for the first time. As usual, Florence was trailing them. Richard had complained to his pa as they left the yard. He had not wanted his five-year-old sister coming with them. After all, they had been eleven. It was enough they were taking John's kid brother. In the end, they had been told to take her. She had fallen asleep before the fishing trip was over. Richard had fussed and said he knew she would be trouble. When they finished Matt was so excited that he rushed over and woke her to show her all the fish he had caught. She had the same tousled look then as she wiped her eyes and opened them to see the catch. After, she smiled and seriously agreed that that was a lot of fish. Matt had run back to John to help him with the poles, and Richard roughly told Florence she'd better get up because he wasn't going to carry her.

Marc remembered how she had stumbled sleepily after them and how Richard's brotherly conscience had won in the end. He handed Marc his pole and string of fish, then strode back to scoop Florence into his arms. He had gruffly informed his little sister that she would have to stay home next time if she couldn't keep up. However, she had given him such an adoring hero worship smile that she went with them almost every time they fished after that.

Marcus was so lost in thought that he hadn't seen Florence disappear into the outhouse. The door soon started to open, so he quickly stood at the front door with his back to the yard and knocked. The door was opened by Alice, who smiled broadly at him and then looked behind him to see her sister coming across the yard.

"Florey, look who's here," Alice shouted, and once she received the startled look she had wanted as Florence looked up on the porch, she said, "Good morning, Marcus. Come on in."

He complied and had just greeted Mr. and Mrs. Cushman when a flushed Florence dashed past him to the back bedroom and shut the door. Her ma almost fussed at her for rudeness and then remembered that Florence and Marcus were not allowed to converse. In a moment, Dawn emerged dressed with every hair in place. She smiled at Marcus.

"Good morning, Marc. I'm afraid Florence wasn't expecting you quite this early. She will be out shortly. Please excuse me." She headed for the front door.

Marc decided that he would definitely wait an additional hour before coming the next time.

The door to the girls' bedroom opened, and a slightly irritated Florence emerged. Her hair was now swept up into a bun. This was not starting out the way Marc had hoped. What made it worse, he couldn't directly apologize to her. Then he smiled to himself because he could indirectly apologize. He turned to Mrs. Cushman, hat in hand.

"I'm sorry that I got here so early. Having the privilege of calling on your daughter this morning caused me to get little sleep last night," he apologized without looking at Florence.

Alan Cushman coughed slightly and turned his head away as his wife glanced his way. Ella looked back at the young man and smiled graciously.

"Think nothing of it, Marcus. I know Florence Elizabeth has looked forward to this day also," she returned.

Florence Elizabeth. He glanced at Florey, who looked shocked that her mother had said it. Marc chuckled inwardly. Yes, he was learning new things already. He raised an eyebrow slightly, and Florence glared at him.

Alan glanced at Marc and Florence. He could see that he was going to have to push them out of the door.

"Marcus, Florence, you are detaining Ella from starting my breakfast. You better see to the milking and egg gathering," he said.

"Of course, sir," Marc said and moved to the door. Florence followed and walked past him through the doorway as he held the door open.

Once they were in the yard, the silence was obvious. Fallen leaves crackled as their feet moved over them on the way to the barn. The horses snickered, and the cow bawled at them as they opened the door. Florence quickly got the stool and bucket, moving to Ol' Rob's side. She patted her side and spoke soothingly to her as she moved to sit beside her.

Florence glanced at Marcus, who was leaning against the stall. Surely, she was allowed to speak to the cow in his presence. It was unnerving having him watch her. She pointed toward the door and then back to the basket that sat beside it, indicating he was to go get the eggs. He shook his head and pointed to himself, her, and Ol' Rob.

Oh, so they would do all the chores together, she thought. Well, they better hurry or her pa would have a fit.

Shaking her head and sighing, she turned back to her task. She worked quickly, but when the pail was half full, she felt a hand on her shoulder, which was quickly withdrawn. She looked up. Marc pointed to himself and then the bucket. So, he wanted to finish. She shrugged and stood up, moving to switch places with Marc. He quickly took her place, reached for the udders, and cleared his throat. She turned to look at him and received a spray of milk in the face! Surprise registered first, but it was replaced by humor as she slowly lifted her fingers to her face to wipe away the liquid. He grinned back at her and chuckled, a deep, hearty sound. In the absence of words, which would have followed under different circumstances, she really relished the warm, masculine sound. She joined in with her own laughter and then gestured to the bucket, crossed her arms, and leaned against the post beside her. He smiled, raised an eyebrow at her, and returned to work. He milked very quickly, and the pail was soon full with frothing warm milk. Marcus stood and pointed to the door. She nodded, and he left to take the pail to the house.

When he returned to the barn, she and the egg basket were gone. He found them beside the barn by the chicken coops. There were several eggs already in the basket. She looked up at the sound of his footsteps, and he shook a finger at her. He took the basket, and she continued to gather the eggs. As she reached for the last one, she noted that it was cracked slightly. She quickly hid it in her hand, pretending that she had not found another one. She turned and pointed to the house. Alice appeared on the porch at that moment.

"Florence, Ma wants those eggs now," Alice said with her hands on her hips.

Marcus quickly crossed the yard, mounted the steps, and gave the basket to Alice. Florence hid her smile as he turned and descended the stairs and made his way toward her. She had never noticed it before, but he had a nice swagger when he walked. Recovering as he neared, she formed a plan for the hidden egg. He smiled as he reached her and gallantly swept an arm toward the house, bowing slightly. She nodded and preceded him toward the steps. However, as they reached the steps and she mounted the first two, she turned back and pointed to the sky. He turned to see the sun starting to emerge when suddenly he felt a tug at the back of the neck of his coat and shirt, followed by something cool starting to slide down his back, and then a female hand hit the object, which caused something slimy to run down his back.

He whirled around, and Florence, eyes dancing with mirth, rapidly ran up the stairs. He followed; then, just as they reached the porch, Florence reversed and ran back down and into the yard. He chased her until they reached the backside of the barn and she held up her hand, which held a white handkerchief she had removed from her pocket. Surrender? She leaned against the barn, breathing hard and smiling. She looked at him to see if he accepted, and her breath caught in her throat. Her stomach was doing that funny thing it used to do when Matt was near her, only this was much worse. He had rendered her incapable of rational thought and normal breath. She knew she had never felt this way before. Marc's eyes were darkened with emotion to a deep forest green. He placed a hand on either side of her head and moved his face within inches of hers. His breath warmed her face. She knew he couldn't kiss her; it was part of the courting agreement. Could he? She glanced at his mouth and then back into his eyes. He glanced down as she nervously licked her bottom lip and then bit it to stop its trembling. Then his gaze locked with hers and held. It seemed like an eternity, and then he suddenly straightened, bowed slightly, waved, and disappeared around the side of the barn. After a dazed moment, Florence followed just in time to see him walking down the road. He shouldn't be leaving, but he was. She slowly made her way to the porch steps and sat down on the bottom one.

That's where Dawn found her when she opened the door.

"Florey, are you well? Where's Marc?" Dawn asked.

"Yes, I'm fine. I think." Florey paused. "Marc had to go change his shirt."

Dawn frowned. "Why?"

Florence turned with a slightly dreamy look on her face.

"I put an egg down the back of his shirt and broke it." She sighed.

Florence stood, mounted the steps, and disappeared into the house before Dawn could respond.

Dawn smiled. This new way of courting just might work for her sister.

∾

The rest of the day was a whirlwind. Alan Cushman waited in the wagon for his daughter. He had already called her two times. What could be keeping that girl? He heard the door slam and heard his wife yell, "Don't slam the door!" as he looked up to see his middle child hurrying down the steps, precariously balancing a freshly made pie. She reached up to hand it to him and then, in a very unladylike manner, climbed onto the seat beside him. She pulled her coat more closely around her and then turned to reach for the pie. As he sat there in astonished silence, she rolled her eyes in exasperation.

"Pa, we are going to be late," she said.

He gave her a stern look and then belied it with a smile. "We certainly are, daughter," he said pointedly.

She looked uncertain for a moment, and then he reached over and patted her hand. They shared a smile, and he reached for the reins. Florence clutched the seat with one hand and the pie with the other as they moved forward. The original plans had been slightly altered. Mrs. Johnson had requested that Florence come to their house for dinner that night instead of Marcus going to the Cushmans'. Emily Johnson felt it was only right since the Cushmans were having everyone for Thanksgiving dinner. She wouldn't have her son being a guest there every night until then.

Lee Johnson and his three sons were in the peach orchard, trying to prepare for the coming frost. All looked up at the sound of the wagon. Jack nudged Marc's elbow, and he hurriedly went out to help Florence off the wagon. She smiled at him and then looked around him and waved at his pa and brothers.

"Good afternoon. I'm going to take this pie inside," she said and then curtsied slightly to Marcus and her pa before heading for the house.

Marc stared after her. He loved her voice! It wasn't one of those high, whiny voices or those lower ones that made it hard to tell gender. It had many hills and valleys. What he liked the most, in addition to its unique tones, were the regional characteristics.

He had heard so many differences in the way people spoke in his travels. Wherever they went in life, they would always sound like home to each other. He had not realized that his pa was speaking to him until he felt his shoulder being given a shake. He turned and found them all smiling at him. He ducked his head, walked over to Will, and punched him playfully as he headed back to the orchard.

Lee looked at Alan.

"What did I tell you?" he asked pointedly.

"I never would have believed it. I'll remember this when Alice starts courting," Alan said.

"Since it looks like it may be another one of my sons doing the courting, I think you better," Lee returned with a knowing smile sent in the direction of his two younger sons. One of which had overheard the last part.

"Pa, what did you say about Alice?" Will asked.

Jack's ears were alerted. "Are they talking about Alice?" he asked his brother.

"Boys, one Cushman daughter at a time," their pa returned.

"Yes, please, boys. I would hate to turn you boys away," Alan seconded.

Alan bade them farewell, and Marcus promised to walk Florence home after supper. Then they quickly returned to their work.

Dinner was wonderful and terrible at the same time. Florence knew the food was delicious, but she barely tasted a bite. She waited for every word out of Marc's mouth as he talked with his family. She wanted to talk to him so badly. She had no idea that he was going through the same torture.

After she helped Mrs. Johnson with the supper dishes, he walked her home. She had treasured the moment when he helped her with her coat. Then they had left the sound of Will and Jack's energetic conversation behind. Now, the cold night air enwrapped them in silence. Florence lifted her face, taking a deep breath of the crisp, refreshing air and smiled. Slowly, she realized that she wasn't nervous; she felt at peace. It was comforting having Marcus, so tall, so strong, walking beside her. It was right. She could hear his even breaths and, as she turned her head, see the cold, smoke-like form of his exhalations in the chilly night air. She lifted her hands, cupped them over her mouth, and breathed warmth into them. She saw him start to reach up to grab her hands, and then watched his hands drop to his sides. He gave her an apologetic look and then stuffed his hands in his pockets dejectedly. They reached the steps of her porch and turned to face each other. Their eyes studied each other for a lingering moment. Then he saw a look pass across her face. He knew that look. She had an idea. He gave her a knowing and warning look. She smiled mischievously and pointed to his pockets. He was confused. She shook her head, pointed to him and then to her hands. He carefully and uncertainly removed his hands from his pockets and held them up. She cupped her hands and then pointed to his. He cautiously imitated her and she nodded. She then did the most peculiar and wonderful thing. She placed her cupped hands just over but not touching his and breathed her warm breath into them. Then, as he held his breath, she removed her neck scarf and wrapped it around his hands. He gazed at her in wonder. She smiled the sweetest smile he had ever seen and then quickly turned and ran up the steps and opened the door. He saw her pause as she turned to shut the door, the candlelight from the house glowing around her, and smiled up at her before she closed the door. Marcus lifted his scarf-covered hands to his face and breathed in deeply. How had he ever merited such a treasure? He looked heavenward and said thank you before he turned to walk home briskly.

❧

The next morning, his foot had just hit the bottom step leading to the Cushmans' porch when the door opened. Alan Cushman stepped out onto the porch, closing the door behind him.

"Good morning, Marcus," Mr. Cushman said as he caught sight of Marcus.

"Good morning, sir," he returned and continued up the stairs but stopped as the older man descended and waved for him to follow.

They walked to the wood pile and both began to gather wood.

Mr. Cushman paused and looked across at Marcus in a way that someone does when they have something to say but aren't quite sure how the other person will react. Marc tensed slightly. Surely, he hadn't changed his mind about letting Florence get married.

"Marc, you know how headstrong Florence can be?"

Marc did not like how this was starting. "Yes, sir. What has she done?"

Mr. Cushman picked up another piece of wood before answering. "Well, it is more something she did before." He saw the concerned look on Marc's face. "Son, it's not that serious. Let's go put this wood on the porch and sit and talk while we wait for my daughter."

Marc breathed out a little. He had called him son, so maybe he was just going to give him some advice. He followed to the porch where they deposited the wood; they sat on the steps together.

Alan pushed his hat back a little and stared forward, arms on knees. "Florence got this strange idea during the war that if she was going to have to do the men's work around here, she shouldn't have to bother with a dress. She found some of Richard's old clothes and started wearing them. Now mind you, this was before I returned home." He glanced sideways at Marc to see how he was digesting the information. The young man's face had a slight smile playing at the corners of his mouth, so Alan continued. "Her mother was scandalized, to say the least. She wrote the whole story to me. Florence chopped wood and even tried to get the crops going until they knew it was futile. Ella said the girl ran all over the place, town and all, in Richard's old clothes. Until one day

176 ~ LANA LYNNE

a troop of our soldiers stopped by and found Florence out doing the chores. She had her hair up under a hat, and they thought she was a boy. They came to the door to inquire about her age to see if she could join up. Ella called Florence over and made her remove her hat. Needless to say, they did not recruit her, and thank the Lord that they were a group of Southern boys who had not completely forgotten their manners. Ella and the girls were gracious and fed them what they could before they left."

Marcus thought about the danger they could have been in as he listened to the story. He thought about Boyd's brother. Then he smiled at the thought of Florence in Richard's clothes. He turned his head toward the man seated on his right.

"I wish I could have seen that," he said.

Then he heard the door open, and as they stood and started to turn, Alan replied, "That wish is about to partially come true."

Marc quickly looked up to find Florence on the porch in some of Richard's cast off clothes. She held her hat in her hands, and to him she did not look boyish at all. He swallowed hard. He certainly did not want her running all over the place in those clothes.

"Daughter, I think that your husband to be is a little shocked by your appearance. Why don't you go change?"

Marc turned to Mr. Cushman. "As long as she brings a dress to change into after chores, I don't mind. This may be more practical for the chores today. We have to go and cut some lumber for Pa to sell in town, chop some more wood for home, work in the orchard, and tend the livestock." He saw Florence's eyes widen briefly, and he and Mr. Cushman shared a knowing glance.

"Very well, Marcus. Please have her home after supper."

Florence quickly came down the steps and stood beside Marc. He turned toward the road and set off with long strides, which had Florence hurrying to keep up with him. Marcus was torn between feelings of amusement and, for some reason, irritation. He glanced at Florence sporting her brother's hat pulled down low on her head. He knew he was irritated more than amused when she started whistling. What did she think he expected her to do today, a man's work? He had wanted her to be with him, and he had planned to show her how strong her future husband was. Now it looked like she wanted to compete. He was frustrated and confused by her.

His Pa and brothers were waiting by the wagon. They were going to go and cut some timber to sell, as well as get some more firewood.

Lee Johnson hid his smile when he saw his son's set jaw.

Will and Jack were a little surprised at Florence's outfit, but not shocked. They had seen her wear it during war time. Her mother and sisters had helped as they could, but none of them had the stamina or strength Florence did. Her habit of preferring the outdoor activities and trailing behind her pa and Richard had yielded benefits. The Johnsons had helped out when they could, but a heavy load had been handled by Florence. Maybe they should explain it to Marc. They looked at their brother and could see he was not happy about the situation. His muscle was twitching in his jaw, and that made up their minds. When he was like this, no one could talk to him, so they just said, "Good morning, Florey and Marc," and jumped up to sit on the back of the open wagon bed.

Florence quickly turned around and sprang up to sit beside them. She looked up at Marc and smiled. It was important to her to let him know that she was a hard worker. She wanted him to be proud of her today. He seemed a little upset at the moment, and she hoped it wasn't at her. Then he frowned in response to her smile and climbed on the wagon seat beside his father.

Her hopes fell and were replaced by bewilderment. She turned to her two future brothers-in-law and whispered, "What's wrong with him?"

The wagon lurched forward, and the threesome grabbed the edge of their boarded seats. Jack shrugged, and Will paused as he tried to understand the degree of his brother's displeasure.

"Maybe he doesn't want his future wife dressing like a boy," answered Will simply.

"Oh." Florence paused. She had never thought about it.

Her ma and Dawn had tried to make her change this morning, but she thought they were being silly.

Marc had watched her climb trees, fish, and anything else in which they would let her tag along. She had thought he would see the practicality of her outfit. Then she had seen her pa talking to him from the window before she went out to meet him and thought everything would be great. She bit her bottom lip and suddenly felt very foolish. Her thoughts were interrupted by Marc addressing his brothers.

"Will, Jack, since Florence came dressed, we will let her split the firewood we cut yesterday, and then she can chop up the rest of the fire logs. That way we can concentrate on cutting the bigger timber for the mill," he said in a matter-of-fact manner.

Marc turned around and watched over the horses' heads in satisfaction. It wouldn't take long for her to apologize to him and just help him if he asked. He failed to see his pa turn his head and wink at his brothers and Florence.

They arrived at the clearing in the woods where they had begun work yesterday. Boyd, John, and Mr. Wilkins were already there. Their properties backed up to each other, so they shared these woods. Boyd was in the process of splitting the Wilkins' part of the firewood. He stopped and shared an amused look with his comrades when Florence hopped off the wagon. He knew Marc was upset when he had not even tried to go back to help her. He wasn't sure what this was about, but he had the uneasy feeling he was about to find out. Marcus strode over to him and fastened a determined look, which bridged no argument, before removing the ax from his hands. Boyd was watching Marc as he turned and approached his future bride then placed the cutting tool in her hands.

Florence Cushman looked upset and determinedly blinked away the moisture in her eyes and gripped the ax firmly as she headed toward Boyd.

Boyd did not like what he saw happening. He had seen women working beside their husbands. Nancy worked beside him. She had helped him and Ben clear their land. At first, he had felt bad because it was hard for her to keep up, and he felt the work she did taking care of everything else was more than enough. But she had told him that if they all did it together it would really be a home, a place they had all worked so they could live as they had dreamed. She had become so strong that by the time he left for war, he felt confident she and Ben could handle it without him. How very wrong he had been. He felt Florence staring at him and realized she had greeted him and was waiting for a response. He turned his most dazzling smile on her and let his cat-like eyes meet hers.

"Good morning, Miss Cushman. I see that you have come dressed for today's endeavors," he drawled loudly, and then in a quieter tone, "Please do me the honor of enlightening me on the subject of your qualifications for this task. Does your intended overestimate you?"

Boyd hoped that his deep, southern gentleman

drawl coupled with what he hoped was his best earth-shattering smile made her feel highly complimented. It should also make her realize Marc was really behaving badly and worthy of any remorse he might feel after this day was at a close. His friend needed to learn to value his future wife. He knew he had had the desired effect when Florence smiled at him in a conspiring manner.

"On the contrary, Mr. Richards, he definitely underestimates me," she stated assuredly and paused. "Let's not ruin his smug certainty of my failure to complete this task."

Boyd hazarded a look at his friend over Florence's shoulder and was given a displeased glare. His gaze returned to the determined young woman before him.

"You have my word as a gentleman, but I warn you, it is not as good as it once was." At her startled look he continued. "Miss Cushman, in your case, you can depend on it. I wouldn't miss my friend learning a lesson. However, if you do need my assistance, I will be happy to oblige." He bowed slightly and made his way to the tree where John and his pa were working.

Florence pulled out her work gloves from her pocket and quickly put them on her hands. She made herself refrain from looking in Marc's direction. Florence wasn't real clear on why he was so mad at her. It was like she had set out to offend him. The one thing she did know was that he had misjudged her intentions. However, since she was not allowed to talk to him, the best thing to do was just finish the work at hand and let him think whatever he liked. If he decided he did not want to marry her that was fine. She was beginning to get angry, and she did not want to be mad at Marc. This morning was nothing like she had dreamed it would be.

The ax head rested on the ground and the handle was propped on her legs as she secured the gloves and her hat. She grabbed the wooden shaft and reached down to pick up a log and place it vertically on the stump where Boyd had been working. Taking a deep breath, she let the firm handle swing upward and then swiftly and accurately came down with a strong stroke, resulting in a loud whack as the log split. The first log was quickly replaced, and a consistent rhythm developed as she worked. She was concentrating so hard on the task before her that she did not notice Marc's initial snort of disdain as she began turn to shock as she continued.

∾

Mr. Johnson walked over to his son and said, "Marc, you were wrong to think you knew Florence so well. As Alan told you, she helped her family to survive. The girls and women had to keep things going. Your brothers and I helped the Wilkins and Cushmans as we could. It was hard."

"I never imagined she could handle an ax this well. I mean, I've seen Ma split an occasional log, but she wasn't able to do it like this," he said with a gesture toward Florence.

"How much like a skunk do you feel, Son?"

"Completely, Pa."

"Good. Now, let's get back to work. These trees aren't falling by themselves."

"But Pa, I think I better go see her."

"Not now. You better let her finish. Besides, you can't really apologize to her. Can you?" His pa's eyebrow lifted, almost in challenge.

Marc felt guiltier than he ever had in his life, and it was all he could do to make himself turn back to the tree they were chopping. He squared his shoulders and began, taking out all his stored up feelings on the tree trunk. The group worked together steadily for four hours with only three short breaks. John brought Florence some water. Boyd had made her remove her gloves for him to check on the blisters he knew would be forming. The first time her palms were just slightly red, but by the second check bubbles had formed. She shook her head and refused to stop, even at his insistence. Boyd had gone to Marc and told him what an idiot he had been. Marc agreed and started toward Florence, but Boyd stopped him.

"She won't stop until everyone's ready to stop. Nancy was like that." He gave Marc a leveling stare as he said, "You had better fix this, and it's going to take words."

Marc returned his gaze. "I had already decided that."

The golden eyes held a glint of satisfaction. "Maybe you haven't gone completely daft."

Marc inclined his head slightly in consideration and grinned apologetically. Boyd headed back to help John and Carl. Marc glanced toward Florence, hoping to find her looking his way, but she had resumed working. Will tapped Marc on the shoulder, and he returned to his labors. The rest of the morning was complete torture for Marc, and he knew he had only himself to blame.

Florence's shoulders and back ached, and her hands burned. Her hair was drenched under her hat. Mr. Johnson called out to stop for the morning and to come back in the early afternoon. Florence straightened and arched her back to stretch her tired muscles. John made his way over to her and, before she could protest, removed the ax from her hands, placed it against the stump, and bodily picked her up and carried her to the wagon.

"John, I can walk," she protested.

"I know, but as your soon to be brother, I can help you if I want."

He had definitely been meant to be her brother-in-law one way or the other, she thought. She smiled tiredly and rested her head against his shoulder. "I guess you can. Thank you."

John felt protective of her and filled with admiration at her morning's work. Dawn had told him how it had been on the home front. They reached the wagon, and John deposited her gently on the wagon seat.

"I'll go get the tools together," he said.

She nodded and then removed her hat and started to remove her gloves. The moment she pulled at the first one she knew the blisters had erupted and the gloves were sticking to her palms. It was going to be painful to remove them.

Marc had been watching her inadvertently all morning. His fists clenched when his friends had taken care of her instead of him. His pa had reminded him that they were not supposed to talk or touch, but he had had enough. He removed his own gloves and tossed them to Jack. He caught his father's eye.

"Pa, I am going to take care of her now. I've learned a hard lesson, courting or not."

All eyes were on him, and no one tried to stop him. He reached the wagon and stood looking at Florence. She was still trying to slowly remove her gloves when he arrived. Wordlessly, he climbed up onto the seat beside her and hesitantly took her gloved hands in his. She stiffened briefly, and his eyes quickly looked at her face. Remorse was written in the expression on his face, and emotional and physical pain were written on hers. He reached for the canteen under the seat and poured cold water into the gloves at the openings. The cooling liquid reached her palms and removed the stickiness of the open blisters. Then he gently removed the gloves. He groaned at the sight of her palms and fingers. He anxiously shared her gaze.

"Florence, I am so sorry," he said humbly.

He could tell she was startled at the sound of his voice.

"Marc, my hands have been blistered before. They will heal," she responded slowly.

"So I've been informed. It seems you are always rising to whatever challenges confront you." He paused and made sure his gaze did not break from hers. "I admire that. I'm apologizing because you came to share whatever chores I had today, and I did not work beside you. We could have finished the firewood in half the time, your hands would not be this blistered, and then you could have rested and watched me try to impress you the rest of the morning." He grinned at the last. He saw her lips twitch slightly, but she wasn't letting him off that easily. His face became serious as he said, "Florey, you have a lot of spirit and determination. It used to exasperate all of us when we were children because you never knew when to stop. However, I now see that perhaps none of us ever took the time to understand your reasons and probably misunderstood them. I know I did today..." He saw her eyes soften a bit, and her mouth opened to speak, but he placed a quieting finger on her lips and shook his head. "I don't want to break your spirit. There are many men who do that to their wives. I've seen it. All for the sake of proving they have the control. Your spirit helps make you who you are. If I let God control me, I'll treat you right, and you will have respect for me. You weren't trying to challenge me today; you were showing how you could help me. Right?" He waited for her nod and continued. "You were always proving you could keep up with Richard, John, Matt, and me so we would let you hang around with us. It's not exactly the same, but close." He shook his head and hit his fist to his knee. "You were so sweet last night, warming my hands and giving me your scarf. How could I have questioned your motives this morning?"

He looked back at her as he felt her reach up, brushing aside the hair that hung across his forehead.

"Richard calls it the snorting bull attitude. An all-male reaction with very little thought behind it," she said, smiling.

He felt himself flush. She made him feel like a schoolboy again.

"So, Miss Florence Elizabeth," he paused in emphasis, and she playfully punched him and then winced at the burning in her palm, "Cushman, am I forgiven?"

She stared at him for a moment before she nodded. "Yes, if you would please take me over to Mrs. Wilkins for some salve. She makes it herself, and it sure made my hands feel better when I did this before."

He had the impulse to hug her but refrained in front of so many eyes. Instead he turned his most charming grin on her, and Florence decided that even Boyd Richards' delightful smile could not compete.

Her knees were jelly. Marc jumped down and reached up for her. He then picked her up and crossed to the Johnsons' wagon.

He turned and called to his pa and brothers, "I'm going to take Florence to get some of Mrs. Wilkins' salve. We will be home for lunch."

An assenting nod was given, and he quickly turned back to Florence. She smiled and handed him the reins, grimacing slightly. The wagon moved forward, heading for the Wilkins' farm.

As the wagon moved out of sight, Boyd quickly removed his gloves and slapped his palm with them with a feeling of satisfaction. He had been a little apprehensive about the compatibility of Marc and Florence at first. Florence had been so sassy and indignant during their first meetings. Now he felt those were great qualities. They made her strong, but not overbearing, because they were balanced with a warm, caring heart. He was happy for his friend and, for the second time that day, had been able to not feel bitter or resentful when he thought of Nancy. He removed his hat and tossed his gloves in it before striding to his horse for his canteen. The water sure tasted good. He heard a scuffle behind him and turned to find Will and Jack wrestling. He watched Mr. Johnson step around them with a short verbal reprimand, which ended the skirmish. The youths jumped to their feet and followed their pa to the Wilkins' wagon, where John and Carl waited. A strange feeling came over him, and he slowly realized he missed Ben. During the past few years, he had reined his emotions so strictly that even his feelings for his brother had been sacrificed. He made a decision and quickly swung up on his horse.

"John, I'm going to town. I'll be back this afternoon," he called and quickly galloped away. He had written to Ben before he left West Texas to let him know where to reach him, as well as sending him half of his last pay. Maybe there would be a letter today.

The town's daily activities were progressing: people and supplies were being unloaded from the river ferry, a stagecoach was unloading in front of the hotel, and work was continuing on the courthouse. Boyd reined his horse in front of the telegraph and post office. As he dismounted, he noted the blue uniforms of the remaining members of the federal troops still posted in the town. A sense of caution and suspicion still overtook him whenever he spotted those Yankee colors. Outwardly, he showed none of his emotions and calmly removed his hat before ducking into the doorway before him. There were two people in front of him getting their mail. He let out a breath as he approached the postmistress. Mrs. Bailey smiled at him as he approached her.

"Mr. Richards, how are you today?" she greeted him.

"Fine, Mrs. Bailey. You are looking lovely today," he returned and was honored to see the little gray-haired lady before him smile with pleasure. "Would you be able to further brighten my day by having a letter for me?"

His heart fell as she frowned slightly, but his hopes were raised when the frown turned into a smile after she reached for a letter from the top of the mail bag.

"This just came in on the stage. I had just opened the bag before you came, so I knew I had seen your name. It just took me a moment to remember where it was," she said as she passed it to him.

"Dear lady, you have brought sunshine to my day. Good day to you." He gave her a broad smile and moved to stand in the shadowed corner of the doorway.

It was so good to see Ben's sloppy script on the address. He opened it quickly and let his eyes scan the contents. A frown creased his brow as he made himself read it more thoroughly a second time. He had just finished when rough, stubby fingers reached and grabbed it from his hands. His hawk-like gaze surveyed a short, stocky soldier standing in front of him

"We are supposed to read all the mail of any former Johnny Rebs under suspicion," the soldier sneered.

"I did not realize I was under suspicion, sir," he replied calmly.

"You are Captain Boyd Richards of Hood's Brigade?"

Boyd's eyes narrowed as he nodded.

The younger soldier lifted the letter to begin reading and glanced up to state, "Then you are under suspicion of still plotting to undermine the Reconstruction efforts of the United States government." The heavy sound of military boots behind him caused the young private to turn and quickly come to attention and salute. "Lieutenant Hawkins, I just discovered this rebel receiving a letter that had not yet been cleared."

The look on the face of Lieutenant Ronald Hawkins indicated he did not want any volatile situations today.

"Thank you, Private. I would like to handle this personally. Dismissed!" He returned the private's salute and took the letter before facing Boyd. He met the amber gaze briefly before turning his attention to the letter. He finished reading and then looked up at the taller man before him with a puzzled expression.

"Captain," he checked himself, "I mean, Mr. Richards, did you finish reading this before the private intercepted it?" The lieutenant continued as Boyd nodded. "Would you truly consider your brother's proposal?"

"I don't intend to only consider it. I intend to do it. If your private had not interrupted me, I would have already telegraphed a reply."

"What profit is it to you? The free labor system they have been trying to establish for former slaves in Texas has been hard to establish. Most have had to sign on as tenants. This helps the landowners. You are obviously a landowner."

"Yes, sir, I am, and taxes have been so high that in order to keep my land, it has forced me to work away from my home. There has been a drought this year. My brother now only has one leg, and his proposition would give him some much needed help in more ways than you can understand."

"The letter says these former slaves were your uncle's in Georgia. Why would they come to you and your brother?"

Boyd did not like sharing private information, but he had no choice. "Lieutenant Hawkins, Ben and I grew up with Martha and Daniel. That's one reason we left Georgia. We did not want to own our friends."

Ronald Hawkins was apparently becoming more confused. "If you felt that way, why didn't you fight for the Union?"

"Yankees think it was all about slavery. My wife and my neighbors were all confederates—some owned slaves, most did not. It was more about loyalty to a way of life. Right or wrong, it was what we knew. Martha and Daniel are our friends. We will help each other."

Lieutenant Hawkins looked back at the letter and then to Boyd. "Your brother doesn't write how your wife feels about this." He took a step backward as the gaze fixed on him turned icy.

"She doesn't feel anything anymore, Lieutenant. She's dead." Boyd saw the information register and held his hand out for his letter. "May I have my letter now?"

HOME ALWAYS BECKONS ~ 193

The letter was held out to him, and as he reached for it, Lieutenant Hawkins asked, "If you or your friends return to Texas, please let me know. I could give you a letter that might be of help in your endeavors."

Boyd did not let his surprise show. He exchanged a look of mutual respect with the lieutenant as he took and folded the letter.

"May I go and send my reply now?" he asked.

The lieutenant frowned and then smiled slightly. "Technically, I am supposed to supervise such action, but let's just say this officer does not find that action necessary in this case. I think there are more pressing matters that need my attention at this time. Good afternoon, sir." He replaced his hat and quickly crossed to and mounted his horse. The golden eyes of the former Confederate soldier who was leaning against the doorway of the telegraph office watched the older officer ride away. Once again, he realized how very little he truly understood about the men he had fought against.

In Texas, Boyd's brother, Ben, gazed at the two crosses beneath the huge pecan tree.

"He's coming home, Nancy and Sam. I know he won't stay, but he's coming. Hopefully, he will stay through planting and harvest. Martha, Daniel, and I need help. There is too much for us to do alone. Adam had to go help his family, with his brothers leaving home and all the tax problems. I promise you

I won't let this place go. Boyd will come home to stay one day." Ben replaced his well-worn hat and turned to hobble toward the house.

Martha was pouring Daniel coffee as he came inside.

"Mr. Ben, you gonna show it to him this time?" Martha asked as he hung his hat on the peg by the door.

Ben sighed deeply and haltingly made his way to where a Bible lay on the small table beside the bed. He picked it up and opened it to where a piece of paper lay folded between the pages of the Psalms. He turned, Bible in hand.

"Yes, Martha, I am. I'll make him read it. He refused and was crazed before. He owes it to her and to himself."

"Lawd knows," she agreed.

Ben read the Psalm 23, his gaze lingering on the words. "Yea, though I walk through the valley of the shadow of death, I will fear no evil: for Thou art with me ... " Before opening the folded page, Ben flipped back to the "Family Record" Nancy had started in the front of the Bible and read the printed date indicating two months before her death, where she had written the date of joining the church and her baptism. He had not been there but had visited with the preacher since then. A smile lifted his lips as he read his own name, as he had written it under hers just this past year. He flipped back to the Psalms and opened the folded page. The handwriting was shaky, and you could tell the lines had been written at different times:

My precious Boyd Boy,
When Sam died, he was with me. Now, He is with me.
I love you.
Nancy
Let him …

The last additional line she had started was not finished. A large ink blot marred the paper. The Bible had been opened and the paper lying in the Psalms where he had kept it when Ben found her. The ink bottles had spilled on the bed, and the pen had fallen from her hand. He had not been able to face it or be comforted by it at first. When Boyd came home, he had handed him the Bible. Boyd flung it back at him without opening it. Now he could share with Boyd and "Let him …" do the comforting.

Daniel's deep voice drew his attention.

"Mr. Ben, come look out the window."

Ben replaced the letter in the Bible and returned it to the table before he crossed to the window where Martha and Daniel stood. A brilliant, multi-hued sunrise lit the sky.

"Don't it take your breath?" Martha breathed.

Ben whispered, "Boyd, my brother, I hope you embrace this new sunrise."

Chapter Eight

The golden warmth from the red overtones of the flames in the fireplace heated John's face as he leaned his head against the mantle, staring into the dance of light and shadows. His heart and mind were troubled for the man who sat behind him awaiting a response. It had taken Boyd two days to approach him after he had sent Ben his reply. Three sets of eyes were boring a hole in his back, and three more sets were darting surreptitiously away from the task of washing the dinner dishes every now and then. He could feel them as he kicked at the ashes a minute longer before turning around. While everyone waited, John let his eyes find Dawn's gaze first. A message passed between them, and she turned back to drying the dishes, which his mother was washing. His gaze skimmed past Marc's bowed head and locked with the eyes filled with guarded expectancy in their amber depths.

"Boyd, I could say I'll think on it, and it would surely need some prayer. Boyd, my heart and mind have already done a little of both in the hours since you told us about it after lunch. Dawn and I were able to talk about it a little before supper. She has left the final decision to me. You are like a brother to me." He paused as he saw his pa swallow hard. "However, it has taken me a long time to come home. There is peace in being here. You are right; it is a time for building a life. Dawn and I will build it here. Couldn't you be the one to work and build up your land with Ben, Martha, and Daniel? I am sure they are only expecting you."

Marc's eyes briefly met Boyd's, and then he got up and walked out the door. It was hard for him to watch Boyd's pain and John's frustration. John was right when things were viewed practically and from a family obligation viewpoint, but when it came to Boyd those things had not applied since the war ended. Marc knew Boyd loved his brother, but he also knew nothing had really changed for Boyd since the last time he had been home. He could hear Boyd and John's voices continuing. He walked to the end of the porch and stared up at the stars. He turned his head as the door opened. Florence shut the door behind her as she wrapped a shawl around herself. Her soft steps brought her to his side. The sky stole her gaze for a moment, and she sighed before looking up at Marc. She found his eyes already on her face and blushed slightly. The night breeze stirred the escaping tendrils of hair against her cheeks. Marc reached a callused finger to lift the dancing, curling strands away at one side. Florence's breath caught in her throat, her eyes never leaving his. His finger then trailed lightly down the hollow below her sculpted cheek bone to gently trace the shape of her soft lips. She was about to think she would never breathe again when he suddenly dropped his hand, placing it in his pocket. He ducked his head and turned away.

Florence exhaled and clasped her hands together in front of her. "Marc, I came out here to ask you something."

He turned slightly, and the look on his face was so masked that she almost ran inside. However, Florence had never run from anything, especially not Marcus.

"So, ask, Florence," he said shortly.

She wished she could know what he was thinking and feeling.

"All right," she began haltingly. "Well, I know Mr. Richards cannot face returning to his farm to stay. I can't say I truly understand that, but in some strange way I know you do. John and Dawn have decided their place is here."

She paused, and he was puzzled. Where was she going with this? The dove gray eyes were earnestly searching his face, and it was getting to him.

"That's right, Florence. What are you trying to ask?" he prompted.

Keeping her eyes on him, she nervously licked her lips and continued in a very soft voice. "Where is our place?"

He frowned. Was she unsure if he would provide for her?

"Florence, I'll build us a house. My pa will let me have a small portion of his land to start—"

Florence sighed and walked to stand beside him, looking out at the yard. He turned and followed her gaze.

"That's not what I mean, Marc." She continued to look outward. "I mean, do we know our place is here in Arkansas, or could we go to Texas?"

Marc wasn't sure he had heard her correctly. He turned her to face him, his hands on her shoulders, and bent his knees so he could look at her on eye level.

"Florey, are you saying you would consider leaving Rockport?"

She nodded before speaking. "I've always been the one my parents had trouble keeping at home."

He took on the tone he used with a skittish colt. "Sweet girl, you've never run much past that special tree of yours. Texas is a lot farther. If we settled there, it would be hard to come back for visits. A farm of our own would take commitment."

Many thoughts raced through her mind, yet all of them brought her back to one thing. When they married, her home would be with him. She had seen his yearning to help his friend on his face when John and Boyd had been talking. He would be going if it wasn't for her. She felt sure of it.

"You want to go to help Boyd, don't you?" she asked.

He straightened and leaned against the porch post. "It's not going to be easy. I just got home. My family won't want me to go this soon." He paused and then nodded. "Yes, I do want to help him and his brother Ben. Florey, the boy is just seventeen years old and has basically had the lone responsibility of running their farm since his return from the war. He's done well, especially with only one good leg, but that young man needs his brother. I know their friends Martha and Daniel are there now, but it's not enough. Please don't think Boyd doesn't love his brother. It's just that being there tortures his spirit, not just because of the death of his wife and son, but because he is running from God. I can't force Boyd to surrender to God, but I can be there for his brother until he truly is ready to come home. He has never given up on me. I wish John and Dawn would go."

"They won't, but you want to, and I want to be with you," Florence said as she shyly put her hand on his arm, "wherever that is. Mr. Richards is a very complex person who I don't understand, but I have been privy to a kindness in him. If you feel the need to go, maybe God is pulling you, showing you our place."

It was at that moment Marcus knew he loved her. There had always been caring, affection, and he had felt a new attraction and appreciation start since he had returned. He had measured it carefully. War, prison, and the lonely trail had taught him caution. He gently stroked her cheek, painfully aware of his chapped fingers against her petal-soft face. The lump that had formed in his throat was choking him, so he swallowed hard and cleared his throat. This was new and untested territory. A frown passed across his features, and Florence bit her lip uncertainly. Marc saw it and pulled her to him, placing his chin on top of her head as he held her close. A sigh and shudder moved her slight form. She shyly nuzzled into his chest. He felt her start to pull back and tightened his hold.

"Florence Elizabeth Cushman, you are a wonder." He pulled back and tilted her chin upward so he could gaze into the windows of her soul. "I love you." He saw the tears begin to glisten in her eyes and had to blink back unaccustomed moisture from his. "I know you still love Matt, so don't feel bad because—"

He stopped talking as a soft finger was placed on his lips. She gazed up at him for what seemed like hours and then slowly rose on tip toes and brushed her lips to his. He was mesmerized. As she settled back onto her feet, she reached for his hands and cradled them in her small grasp.

"Marcus Elias Johnson." She smiled at his surprise. "Your ma and I have talked." Then she continued. "For a man of vast experience, you sure are dense!" A playful yet tender smile danced across her mouth. "I have realized some things as well. My love for Matt will always remain, but it was a little girl's love that never had the opportunity to blossom. That was God's will. Marc, there have been many conflicting emotions within me since you returned." She shook her head when he started to interrupt, then ducked her head and whispered, "I love you, too."

His voice was husky as he tilted her face back up, letting his imploring gaze lock with hers. "Please, say that again."

The small flame that danced within her young heart exploded and reflected in her voice. "I love you, Marc."

Joy and a sense of completeness settled upon them. He grinned like a schoolboy. "You really want to go to Texas?"

A smile spread brightly across her face and she nodded. "Yes, let's go tell Mr. Richards."

"You better call him Boyd."

Heads turned with questioning eyes as they came through the door. Boyd was still by the fireplace, and the young couple quickly made their way to him. Marc pulled Florence to stand in front of him, his hands resting on her shoulders as he met the now puzzled, ever golden eyes of his friend.

Before anyone had a chance to speak, Marc announced, "Florey and I will go to Texas with you, Boyd."

"Florence, no! You can't!" Dawn blurted out. "You can't be that far away."

Florence turned to her sister, John, and his parents. "Yes, I can," she said calmly. "I suggested it. Dawn, I've always been hard to keep at home. You and Alice always have stayed close."

Her sister's eyes filled with tears, and she started

to go to her, but Mrs. Wilkins and John had already crossed to comfort Dawn.

Mrs. Wilkins' eyes found Florence's. "Child, you have been like a daughter to me, and now your sister will be my daughter-in-law. I am so proud of you! Follow your heart and remember, God is in control."

That was the blessing she needed to hear at that moment. She turned back to find Boyd watching her intently.

"Miss Cushman, I mean, Florence, are you absolutely sure?" asked Boyd.

She straightened her shoulders, head high, as she declared, "I am, Mr. Rich … Boyd."

Boyd's attention shifted to his friend in silent appreciation. The sound of Mr. Wilkins clearing his throat broke the moment.

"You young people need to consider some things. Marcus, you better get Mr. Cushman's blessing before you confirm these plans. The next thing to consider is Thanksgiving is upon us. The first holiday our families have all been able to celebrate together in years, and I would hope you would still be here for Christmas, but with the possibility of icy weather, I hate to say it, but you may want to leave after Thanksgiving to be safe in your travel. Boyd, you did say your brother needed help before spring, right?" He continued at Boyd's nod. "Giving thought to travel time, safety, and conditions is wise. Now, Marcus, this is going to be a shock to your family as well as Florence's. I suggest you mind how you tell them, and Boyd needs to be there."

Somberness settled over all of them. Marc could picture his parents' faces, and a lump formed in his throat. He saw Dawn cross to Florence and embrace her. Uncertainty filled him, and he was unsure if he could leave Arkansas again. He felt a hand on his shoulder and turned his head toward Boyd, who nodded toward John. John motioned them both toward the door.

The three friends walked out on the porch. Then John went down the steps and headed around the corner of the house. Boyd and John followed. John did not stop until he reached the large tree with the marker for his brother in front of it.

"Boyd, I had to come home and face this, but coming home also brought me more joy and peace than I ever could have imagined. You need to go home and truly deal with losing Nancy. Quit running and quit having other people handle what you should be handling."

The sound of the soft wind blowing seemed overwhelming as the tension of the moment grew without a response from Boyd. Boyd was filled with anger and hurt, but he knew John was right; yet he also knew he could not live in East Texas again permanently. He understood his brother needed help or he would lose all they had ever worked for since they left Georgia. He wanted someone he could trust, and these two men with him at this moment were the only ones worthy. There was also something else he knew. John had a spiritual life he couldn't understand. He swallowed hard.

"John, you're right, and I will in time. My brother needs help now."

John hit his fist into his hand in frustration. "Boyd, Marc needs to stay home. It took us too long to get here."

As Marc listened and watched his friends, a strange peace settled on him. He sent a silent prayer upwards before he spoke. "John, I don't know why, but Florence and I are to go to Texas. I'm sure of it. Like your ma said, God is in control." He met John's gaze and received a reluctant nod and, at Boyd's skeptical grimace, added, "Whether we accept it or acknowledge it, he is. We are going, John. I'm leaving you to look out for my two kid brothers. Think you can handle it?"

John sighed, shook his head, and then grinned. "I'll give it my best."

Boyd couldn't believe John would accept it that easily. "You gentlemen confound the mind. I do not understand."

Marc and John grinned, white teeth reflecting in the darkness, and quoted Proverbs 3:5–6 in unison: "Trust in the Lord with all thine heart; and lean not unto thy own understanding. In all thy ways acknowledge Him and He shall direct thy paths."

John clasped Boyd by the shoulder and bent close to his face. "I'm praying for you whether you like it or not."

Boyd shrugged him off and headed for the house. Marc and John followed.

の

Alice thought it sounded like an adventure and said so repeatedly until she was sent back to bed. Mrs. Cushman glared at Marcus and said that it was entirely his fault. Then she blamed her husband for allowing Florence to become engaged, and finally, Florence was to blame. As a group, they were charged with purposefully conspiring to make her life harder by moving her daughter away. Florence then said that her mother still had Dawn and Alice. This was met by tears and her mother going to bed, vowing to not get up until the New Year. Dawn and Florence followed her to her room to try and calm her.

The room was suddenly quiet. Mr. Cushman and Marc sat facing each other at the table. The older man's gaze searched the face of the younger. Florence had always been the one he had silently feared would leave Arkansas. One of the reasons he had chosen Arnold was to keep Florence close to home, but after what had happened with Arnold, his wife had considered sending Florence to relatives in Virginia who would send her to college. Florence would have hated it. He had been hopeful that Marcus Johnson would remain home after so many years away, yet knowing there was always the possibility of the young man wanting to roam. He had always been an adventurer. How was he to entrust the care of his daughter to another human being in a place in which he would not be able to be present? It had been an easier thought when he knew they would be in the same community. Flashes of Florence as a baby, toddler, and little girl to present went through his mind. His throat constricted with emotion, and he looked down. Then, flashes of Marc as a child playing with Richard, working in the fields with his pa, and then marching off to war also exploded in his memory. He looked up and found Marcus waiting uncertainly for a response. He shook his head, stood, and went to check on Ella.

Marcus sat at the table with his insides churning. Things had not gone well since Florence and he had left the Wilkins's. They had gone to his house first. His brothers were mad at him, and he openly let Florence see tears course down his face as his mother had cried. Then his parents, in their characteristically unselfish way, had given them their blessing. Now he couldn't even get Mr. Cushman to talk to him.

The front door burst open, causing him to lift his head as Richard entered. His friend's face was almost as red as his hair. He was furious.

"John just came by to tell me your new plans. How could you even consider this? I will not let you take my little sister away!" Richard ranted.

Marcus braced himself as Richard pulled him out of the chair and pulled him to the door.

"Get out, Marcus! Go ahead and go to Texas! I don't know how Boyd Richards has come to mean more to you than any of your other friends and family. I'm done."

"Richard, I am here to speak to your father and am not leaving until he tells me." Marc tried to step around Florence's irate brother. His feelings for her went beyond his feelings for any other friend at this point.

"I say you're done," said Richard evenly right before he punched Marcus, knocking him through the still open door onto the porch.

Marcus reacted quickly, springing to his feet and pulling Richard down the steps into the yard before he returned his blow. Both men were full of adrenaline and dredged up grievances. They did not even notice when the rest of the Cushman family appeared on the porch to watch. Richard had always been a good fighter, but Marcus always bested him during their childhood skirmishes. Finally, Florence's voice broke through as he gave her brother one last punch, knocking him soundly to the ground. He looked up to see the small audience that had gathered, including Florence, who was being held back by her father. He dropped his fists as he took ragged breaths then reached down to offer Richard a hand. It was knocked away in refusal.

"Ella, take the girls back into the house," said Alan Cushman as he ambled slowly down the steps. His halting gait brought him to stand beside the two young men. He reached down and helped Richard to his feet. "That's enough, Richard. I thought the war had given you your fill of fighting. That fighting wasn't a true choice. This is. Haven't we endured enough? It's almost like we are perpetuating the way of living the War made normal. I don't want Marc and Florence to go anymore than you do, son, but as I watched the two of you fighting, I knew that is exactly what should happen. The good Lord must have plans for them in Texas. Now, go in the house and let your mother tend you before you go home and scare poor Jenny."

Richard sent Marcus one more look of resentment before complying with his pa's request. Alan Cushman led Marcus over to the horse trough.

"Splash your face a time or two and we'll talk."

Mr. Cushman propped against the corral fence to rest his war-injured knee as he watched Marc. Marc finished, shaking the water out of his hair and gingerly touching his swelling, bruised face. The man who would be his father-in-law finally spoke after a few more minutes of silence.

"Marcus, I could get you to promise me you'll take care of her and be good to her as many fathers before me have. I also know that those promises have many interpretations." He caught the look of confusion on Marc's moonlit face and laughed. "You don't know what I'm getting at. Well, let me try again. Promises are easy to make and harder to keep. I know—my wife was young and left a comfortable life in Virginia to come here with me. She wanted to come and has worked beside me all these years. She's only seen relatives of hers a few times since we married. As the years passed, we had children, the farm, times have been good, and they've been hard. The war was especially hard, and these times after it have been

210 ~ LANA LYNNE

difficult. The reason I'm telling you this is because I made a mistake through the years I don't want you to make. Ella became bitter and harder through the years because I took her for granted. I didn't take the time during each day to find out what she felt and thought beyond the responsibilities of life. I quit seeing the girl I had married and became accustomed to the roles she held and completed. It hit me the night of the dance. She startled me, and I saw the woman I loved. Marcus, don't break Florence's spirit, her dreams, or her heart by not giving her your time and attention beyond the everyday things of life. Tiredness of the body and mind at the end of the day are one thing. Fatigue and sorrow of the heart and spirit are another. Love her as the good book says, 'As Christ loved the church.' You will be answering to him if you don't."

The enormity of the responsibility he was about to have settled on Marcus. It was frightening in a way he had never experienced. The closest thing he could compare it to was when he had been responsible for men under his command during the war. It had settled hard on him if he lost any. Then again, the two were totally different. Florence would be his alone. She would look to him, after God, for provision and protection. He thought about Boyd and suddenly could catch a glimpse of the remorse and grief he felt about Nancy.

He felt Mr. Cushman's eyes on him and met his gaze. An expectancy, which demanded a reply, was on the older man's face.

"Yes, sir," replied Marc, his Adam's apple nervously moving up and down.

Alan Cushman's gaze narrowed, and he reached out a hand to jerk Marc forward by the back of the neck.

"Son, if you are unsure at all, you better tell me now. It would be better for—"

"No, sir!"

Courage and certainty welled up in him just as the delightful sound of Florence's shouting came from the house. Poor Richard! It somehow produced an invisible connection Marc could feel, and he smiled, love burning brightly inside of him. His gaze boldly met Alan's.

"Florence is the only one I want for my wife. She knows where I've come from, who I am, and I know her. I will spend the rest of my days using all my strength and breath to make us a life." He paused as he heard the door of the house open. "Treasuring her as my gift and giving back to her each day is my goal."

Florence came out of the house, shutting the door behind her. Alan put out his hand. "I'm depending on it." Marcus reached out to clasp the strong, weathered hand.

"So, how many horses are you trading for me, Pa?" Florence smiled as she moved to her father's side and put an arm around his waist as she looked up at him.

Alan shared his daughter's smile. "Actually, none. Marc and I find the most valuable thing is you," he said playfully, touching a finger to her nose. "However, I would like to help you two out a little as a wedding present."

Marc wanted to refuse, given the difficulties of the times in which they found themselves, but he knew he would never want to dishonor the man who stood across from him. His voice was gruff. "Thank you, sir."

Florence reached up and hugged her father. "Thank you, Pa," she said, placing a kiss on his cheek.

"Sir," Marc broke the moment, "I need to be heading home. With your permission, I would like to speak to Florence for a moment."

"Certainly. Just don't be too long," Alan said, stepping away from Florence. "I'll go check on your ma and Richard."

Florence turned toward Marc, reaching up to gingerly touch his face. "Are you all right? I let Richard know it was not his decision."

Marcus covered her hand as it examined his face and kissed it impulsively, then grimaced at the pain that even that small movement caused. "I've had worse beatings. It's just been awhile. I'll be fine, especially since your pa has just given me permission to take you to Texas."

Florence squealed and spun around in the yard.

The brisk night air felt refreshing as it washed over them. The leaves were dancing in the night air, several spiraling downward as they left the mooring of the branches. Marcus saw mischief and delight fill her. She ran toward the pecan tree at the edge of the house. "Come on!" she called over her shoulder. There was a low branch from the fork of the tree trunk, which she was able to reach and swung up just as Marcus reached the base. She giggled and scrambled to the next branch.

This was the girl he remembered, and he was delighted! He felt the years melt away and swung up after her in spite of his battered state. She was sitting in the apex of two branches, feet dangling with playful movement under her dress. He shook his head and smiled as he reached her.

"I don't know another young woman who could climb a tree in a dress like you do," he said, positioning his foot on a strong branch and holding onto the branch above his head with one hand. He surveyed the ground looming a distance beneath them and chuckled. "I don't know anyone who could get a man of my age to climb like this. Are we crazy?"

Her eyes twinkled at him like the stars above them in the night. How could he not love her? He marveled at God's wisdom and timing. The need to be closer to her overtook him. Assessing the precarious conditions of being in a tree, he decided the branch that was holding Florence would not hold them both. He held out his free hand to her. "Florey," he beckoned in a tender voice. She hesitated and then cautiously joined him. He steadied her, and she grabbed the branch he was holding with one hand. Their proximity was close given the tight quarters of the tree. The warmth of his breath touched her face, and she could feel the uneven breaths he was taking. She lifted her face to look at him and gasped as his lips softly covered hers. He lifted his head to gaze at her. His free arm held her steady at the waist, and her free arm held onto his back and waist.

"I am so thankful for you," he said.

She smiled shyly. "You're welcome, I mean," she stammered and in the frustration reached to give him another tenderly placed kiss. This was the most vulnerable either had felt in their lives. Marc sighed and hugged her to him. There was so much he wanted her to know. He smelled the freshness of her hair and pulled back slightly, watching his footing, to view her face.

"Florey, there is something I want to talk about, but I don't want to offend you or embarrass you." He watched a look of puzzlement then understanding cross her face.

She shifted uncomfortably. Surely he wasn't going to actually discuss what she thought he was going to discuss. People did not talk about those things. At least she didn't think they did. Her ma had told her in a very embarrassed and short way about things when she got her first monthly flow, besides the fact of being raised on a farm. She looked at all the limbs above his head, not wanting to look into his eyes.

"My ma has talked to me. I don't think we are supposed to talk about it." She paused and glanced imploringly at him. "Please."

This was very awkward, and Marc really did not know how to continue, but he knew he must. "Florey,

I'm sure she did. It's not really that, but in a way it is. You see, there is something I need you to know."

His voice was so serious; she suddenly wondered why this was so important. A multitude of thoughts raced through her mind, and then she remembered the stories she had heard about some of the men's injuries after the war. Her gaze sought his.

"Marc, were you injured in … " she started then cleared her throat, too embarrassed to continue.

He looked puzzled and then started to chuckle.

She didn't think this was funny. She started to pull away. "I think I'll go in now."

He stopped her and smiled gently. "No, please, I'm really making a mess of things." He sighed deeply before continuing. "No, I was not injured in that way. How do you know about such things?"

She blushed. "Eloise, my school friend, had this cousin."

He shook his head. His right arm was cramping from holding onto the upper limb. "Could we change arms? Here, I'll go first," he said and removed his left hand from her waist, moving it to the limb above his head, and replaced it with his right hand. "Now, you." She made the same adjustments.

"Now, Florey," he began firmly, "please let me get through this. It is important. During the war, many of the soldiers sought whatever women were available to them. Some contracted horrible diseases. I never did those things."

She was embarrassed, but then he saw something

tender begin to flicker across her face. She returned his gaze and asked quietly, "And after the war?"

The air was electric in expectancy between them. He did not hesitate. "No, not ever."

He watched as the enormity of his revelation settled on her. "Why?" she asked.

He looked away briefly, gathering his thoughts, and then back as he said, "At first and now, it was and is because of being brought up to know that's not what God wants for us until marriage occurs. But during the angry and confused years of bitterness, it was because I didn't want to get close to anyone in any way. Boyd and John also helped. Boyd was so faithful to Nancy, and then he was just in self-isolation. Now, I can't speak for all his actions, but anyway. I wanted to wait." He paused, and his eyes pierced her heart with the love she saw there. "And I am glad. The only memories I want to have in that area are ones we will create as husband and wife." As he spoke the last, he noticed moisture on her cheeks and bent to kiss them away.

The sound of footsteps on the porch drew their attention.

"Florey, where are you?" Dawn called.

"Up here!" Florey replied.

A rustle of skirts was heard as Dawn came to the foot of the tree and peered up. "What in the world?" she exclaimed and then started laughing. "I don't want to know. Florence you better come in now or Pa will be out here."

"Just a minute!" called Florence and shared a

quick look with Marcus. He scrambled down and reached up to help her.

Dawn grinned at them and said, "Goodnight, Marcus," before making her way inside.

Marc caught Florence's hand as she headed toward the porch, and she slowed her pace to walk companionably with him. He walked her up the stairs and to the door.

Florence reached up to tenderly stroke his strong but swollen cheekbones and well-defined jaw. "I love you, Marcus Johnson. Thank you for being the boy I've always known and for becoming so much more in the man you've become."

He reached up and tucked the curling tendrils, which had escaped, behind her ear. The emotions coursing through him were so overwhelming that he had no words. He kissed her lightly on the forehead and then softly covered her mouth with his own. When he pulled away, her eyes fluttered open and she sighed. He knew exactly how she felt.

"Goodnight, Florey. We will meet with Boyd and our families tomorrow. We have a quick wedding to plan if we are to get on our way to Texas," he said, stepping away from her. She didn't answer but continued to stare at him as if dazed. He couldn't help feeling pleased. "Florey, go inside."

Florence turned, opened the door, just as Richard stepped out onto the porch.

"Florence, it's going to be just fine. I'm done fighting. Now go inside. I'll make sure this man you've chosen gets home without mishap," said Richard at his little sister's look of unease. "Pleasant dreams, sis."

"Go on, Florey. I'll see you tomorrow," urged Marc.

They watched her close the door after giving one last loving look at Marcus and a glance of warning to her brother. Marcus eyed Richard, waiting. Richard heaved a deep sigh.

"Care for an apology for the way I handled the news?"

Marc looked at his friend with a rueful smile. "Sure, but only if you'd care for an apology for excluding you from the meeting at the Wilkins."

"Let's walk, my friend," said Richard with a nod.

Their friendship was worth preserving, and they were soon to be family. It was the first time in many years they had roamed these roads at night together; just the two lifelong friends walking and talking all the way home.

The next day, final plans were made. They would marry the Sunday after Thanksgiving, and a nice additional plan had been settled. It would be a double wedding. John and Dawn knew Florence and Marcus would not be able to return for their wedding, so it was arranged with their preacher to unite the best friends to the sisters they had chosen as their brides in one service.

The knowledge of the shortage of remaining

time together and the blessedness of having all family together after so many years made Thanksgiving very special. It was a day where every minute was treasured as precious.

Richard stared at his little sister holding his son, her nephew, and wished he could have a picture of this moment forever. He smiled, at least his pa and Mr. Johnson had been able to arrange for a picture to be taken of the families the coming Saturday before the wedding on Sunday. He saw Marcus coming over to him and smiled at his friend.

"Are you ready to be my brother by marriage?" Marcus asked with humor.

"Well, we have a history of fighting like brothers. I guess I'll have to force myself." Richard punched his arm and then added seriously, "I wish you two could stay here."

Marcus nodded and then watched Florence and Jenny with David. "I'll take good care of her, Richard."

The red-haired man stared soberly at him. "I know. I just hope we will be able to see you again."

A determination burned inside Marcus. "We will make that happen with God's help," he pledged.

Richard held out his hand. "I will hold you to that promise."

By Saturday they had the wagon packed. Marcus and Boyd had bought a team of horses to pull it. Marc's mustang would be tied to the back, and Boyd would ride beside them. Marcus had tried to make sure his brothers were fully involved with all the preparations for the trip. Both had been very angry about him leaving at first, and then they both saw it as a future excuse to travel outside of Arkansas.

They were headed in to dinner that night when they saw two horses approaching the house. The riders were in uniform.

"Mr. Richards," Lieutenant Hawkins addressed Boyd, "I've come to inform you that a small detachment and I will be accompanying you to the East Texas area."

Marcus stiffened, but before he could say anything, Boyd stepped forward.

"Sir, I can't think why such diligence would be necessary," he drawled calmly.

"Not necessary, but advisable. You see, I volunteered to take the detachment so I could be sure any problems of a military nature which might occur on your journey would be handled well," Lieutenant Hawkins said seriously.

Boyd suddenly understood that the Yankee was a friend. He smiled slowly and clicked his heels together. "We thank you, sir."

The officer nodded. "We will be outside the church, ready to move out following the service." He then reined his horse around, followed by the other soldier, and left.

Marcus shook his head. "I never thought I'd see the day you were obliged to a Yankee."

Boyd shrugged and headed for the house.

The night before the wedding ceremony was filled with exhaustingly exhilarating tasks. It was well past their normal bedtime before anyone in the Cushman household finally dressed in their nightclothes in preparation for sleep. Florence had handed Marcus the one last trunk her ma had helped her pack after dinner. She firmly ignored his protests about there not being any more room on the wagon and sweetly pacified him with a kiss before he returned home for an evening with his parents and brothers. Their ma had fussed over their wedding dresses and items needed for the big day. Dawn and Florence had been allowed to bathe first before the rest of the family. They were quickly joined by Alice as they sat by the fire to let their hair dry.

"I know one reason to be glad you are both getting married and moving out of the house—I get to have the tub with the hot water first!" Alice grumbled as she squeezed between them beside the hearth.

Dawn and Florence looked at each other and laughed.

"Now, Alice, just think about Ma and Pa. They are bathing after you," said Dawn.

Alice looked grimmer. "I know, but Ma did just pour two more kettles of hot water in the tub as I was getting out. You two got the best, I got barely tolerable, and they get tolerable. I know, I know, I'm just awful."

"No, you're not, Alice. Cold is what you are.

Come here, little sister, and let me towel your hair a bit more. Mine's barely damp now," offered Florence as she adjusted so Alice could sit more fully in front of her by the fire.

Alice complied, and all was silent for a few moments as Dawn stared thoughtfully into the dancing flames and Florence toweled and combed her little sister's hair.

"Florey?"

"Yes, Alice?"

"What were you writing on your old school slate today?"

"What was I ... ? Alice, were you following me?"

Her little sister turned her head with guilt framing the deceptively innocent blue eyes.

"Don't be mad, Florey. I saw you sneak out to your tree and wanted to watch you sit there one more time," Alice explained sweetly before uncontainable curiosity overcame her once again. "What were you writing?"

Florence blushed as she caught Dawn's interested gaze above their curious sister's head. "Well, I," she hesitated and then sighed as she confided in them, "I was practicing writing 'Mrs. Marcus Johnson.' Isn't that silly?"

"No, dear, it's not. I did that many days before I wed your father."

All three girls turned in surprise at their mother's voice and confession. Ella Cushman smiled at her three girls. "Yes, I was young and in love like you." Their mother advanced into the room and joined them as she sat in her rocking chair. She proceeded to share short vignettes of her courtship with their father. Florence grew more amazed as each one shared added color and depth to the woman before her. The woman she thought she knew had a past she only had known cursory points about until now. She found she had much in common with her mother. Her mother had left Virginia to move to Arkansas with their father at her same age. As Florence pondered this, she realized part of her mother's reluctance for her to move was because she knew all too well how limited opportunities to visit really would be. All this time, Florence had thought she was a nuisance to her mother. Her mind whirled as clarity came and her eyes filled with tears. She noticed her ma's narrative had stopped and looked up to find her mother gently watching her. It only took Ella opening her arms slightly. Florence rose and was lovingly harbored inside the maternal embrace. Her sisters quietly surrounded them to share in the mother-daughter circle, which was woven with invisible cords much deeper than the limitations of physical expression. Alan Cushman lingered in the shadows for a moment to treasure the sight of his family before he turned and quietly retired to bed, knowing tomorrow would change their lives forever.

Sunday morning was clear and crisp. Dawn was radiant in her mother's lace wedding dress, and Florence looked like a princess in the simple but classic ivory cotton dress of Mrs. Wilkins'. Both dresses had been tried by the young women, and the sizes made the decisions with little need for alterations. It seemed fitting, and in a strange way Marcus felt he had Matt's blessing.

Marcus and John stood nervously at an angle to the preacher, flanked by their fathers, Will, Jack, and Boyd. Alice moved to stand opposite of them. Their focus was arrested by the sight of Alan Cushman escorting his daughters, one on each arm, down the aisle. The strength of the love radiating between all in the church washed over the townspeople and family present. John's throat caught at the angelic sight of his golden-haired bride coming toward him. His hands were moist as she transferred to his arm and gazed up at him. Marcus was speechless. Florence's gray gaze had locked with his as she approached, and he was hypnotized. Alan Cushman kissed both his daughters, and then moved to sit with his wife.

Boyd heard the vows exchanged in a surreal haze. He was present but at the same time wasn't. The years had fallen away. He was in the small church in Georgia, gazing down at Nancy in her simple calico dress. She didn't have a real wedding dress. His uncle did not approve, so only the two of them, Ben, and the preacher were present. Her chestnut hair and hazel eyes had glistened with love. They had both been just kids. It had seemed so simple, and he had thought he could conquer the world. He grimaced; instead it had conquered him. Reality shook him as he watched his friends place rings on their brides'

HOME ALWAYS BECKONS ~ 225

fingers. *There has been enough bad. Let this start a new, good period,* he thought. Then he realized his thought had been close to a prayer. He heart was pricked, and he felt vulnerable and quickly suppressed the feelings in his mind and heart. He hugged Dawn, Florence, and shook his friends' hands as the service ended before heading outside.

Lieutenant Hawkins and his detachment were there as promised. Boyd quickly thanked everyone and said good-bye before mounting his horse. He now could focus on the long journey ahead.

It only took less than fifteen minutes after they had changed clothes for Florence and Marcus to finish their good-byes, the longer ones having already been said the previous night.

Florence wore a heavy green travel dress made by Mrs. O'Neal as a wedding gift. It was well made, and as the cooler autumn winds freed the last lingering tree leaves to join the swirl of crisp piles below, she was grateful for the garment's substance. Marc grinned happily at her as he easily swept her off her feet and lifted her up to deposit her gently onto the wagon. She smoothed away her autumn colored curls as the wind swirled by and smiled down at him. He climbed quickly to join her, laughing as she steadied herself on the wooden seat, which creaked in protest at their movements.

As the wagon began to move, Florence felt tears coursing down her face. Rockport was all she had ever known—the people, the land, her home. Even during the chaos of war, it had been a constant, a stronghold. Now she had to let go and move into the unknown. Even though she was at peace in her heart, watching their families wave and blow kisses was hard. This was real. This was change. This was becoming an adult. It was a little scary, and it hurt. Then she felt Marcus's arm around her waist, pulling her to sit closer to him.

"Are you going to be able to do this, Mrs. Johnson?" he asked.

She thrilled at the sound of her new name and met his warm gaze. Her heart calmed and warmed.

"Yes, Mr. Johnson, I am," she responded with a warm and sure smile.

She briefly leaned her head on his shoulder, and he brushed her head with a quick kiss before they turned to get a final look at their families. Memories were silently dancing in the smiles, tears, and waves. Marcus squeezed Florence's hand as they set their faces toward the road leading to their future.

Research Resources

Ashmore, Harry S., Arkansas, *A Bicentennial History,* W.W. Norton and Co., Inc., New York, American Association for State and Local History Nashville, 1978, Chap 7–10, pp. 68–109.

Haines, Francis, *Horses In America,* Thomas Y. Crowell Co., New York (Estab. 1834), 1971, p. 164.

Douglas, C.L., *Cattle Kings of TX,* Branch-Smith, Inc., Ft. Worth, TX , 1939 Cecil Baugh and 1968 Mrs. C.L.Douglas.

Steele, Philip W., and Cottrell, Steve, *Civil War in the Ozarks,* Pelican Publishing Co., Gretna 1998.

Vandiver, Frank E., 1001 *Things Everyone Should Know About the Civil War,* Doubleday Publishing, a division of Random House, Inc., New York, New York 10036.

Websites:

www.VictorianElegance.com/1800.htm/

"The Civil War in Arkansas, Third Arkansas, Third Arkansas Infantry, Regiment, CSA- A Brief History," pp.1–2, and "Third Arkansas Regiment Infantry, CSA, Company F- Hot Springs Hornets," P.P 1–18., www.insolwwb.net/~egerdes/3rd-his.htm/, site visited 2/27/00.

The Handbook of Texas Online, "Hood's Texas Brigade,"

http://www.tsha.utexas.edu/handbook/online/articles/view/HH/qkh2.html, site visited 2/26/00 and 8/17/00

Morgan, James *"Mounted But Not Mounted" The Confusing Terminology of Artillery*, p. 1–5, *"Green Ones and Black Ones" The Most Common Field Pieces of the Civil War* "Shotgun's Home of the American Civil War, first published, January 7, 1997, web master: Dick Weeks., www.civilwarhome.com visited site2/18/00.

"Weapons of the American Civil War" ,pp. 3–4, Shotgun's Home of the American Civil War, first published, January 7, 1997, web master: Dick Weeks., www.civilwarhome.com visited site 2/18/00; Sources cited on web page; The Civil War Society's "Encyclopedia of the Civil War and Mark M. Boatner's "Civil War Dictionary"

"Boys in the Civil War" and "The Ten Costliest Battles of the Civil War", Shotgun's Home of the American Civil War, first published, January 7, 1997, web master: Dick Weeks., www.civilwarhome.com visited site 2/18/00 & 8/17/00.

Fort Delaware Society, P.O. Box 553, Delaware City, DE 19706; www.del.net/org/fort/, site visited 2/13/00.

Howerton, Bryan R., information from e-mail regarding the 3rd Arkansas Regiment Infantry-Prisons of War, Howerton @cswnet.com, 2/27/00.

Shanghai and the Pierce Ranch History "The Pierce Ranch," pp.1–3,

http://www.karankawa.com/his.htm, visited site 10/30/05.

"Princess Style" (dress designs for 1860s), http://www.britannica.com/bcom/eb/article/0/0,5716,62972+1+61413,00.html, Site visited 5/20/00.

Bisonnette, Anne, Curator, "Bissonnette on Costume Time Search; The Nineteenth Century: 1860 to 1869", Kent State University Museum, hip: www.kent.edu/museum/anne/bissonnette/3timesearch/tsnineteenth/1860 ... /1860–1869.htm, visited site 5/20/00.

Information from Research from Malvern Chamber of Commerce, Brenda Matthews:

Goodspeed History of Arkansas, Chapter XVIII, p. 319–327.

The Heritage, Vol. II, "Early Roads of Hot Spring County" p. 33–39; IV, "The History of Hot Springs County" p. 3–4 , "Arkansas Toothpicks" p.14; Volume V, "Brief History of Hot Springs County, Arkansas" p. 96–98 and "history of Hot Spring County, Arkansas"; Volume VII, "Old Rockport gets Two New Bridges" p. 109—111; Volume VIII, "Old Rockport Where The President Worships Wednesday" p. 109–115; Volume XV, "Chronology of Battle Engagements of the Hot Spring County

Hornets-(Rockport Volunteers) p. 138–139, published by the Hot Springs Arkansas Historical Society; Volume XXIV "When Our Major Rivers Had No Bridges", Source Unknown, P133 and "You May Hear Some More About Rockport", Source Unknown, p.134.

Malvern Daily Record's 50th Anniversary Book

Research Information from Azalee Duke:

Ferguson and Atkinson, 1966, *Historic Arkansas,* p.p. 33–35, p.p. 127–130.

listen|imagine|view|experience

AUDIO BOOK DOWNLOAD INCLUDED WITH THIS BOOK!

In your hands you hold a complete digital entertainment package. Besides purchasing the paper version of this book, this book includes a free download of the audio version of this book. Simply use the code listed below when visiting our website. Once downloaded to your computer, you can listen to the book through your computer's speakers, burn it to an audio CD or save the file to your portable music device (such as Apple's popular iPod) and listen on the go!

How to get your free audio book digital download:

1. Visit www.tatepublishing.com and click on the e|LIVE logo on the home page.
2. Enter the following coupon code:
   1c4d-26f7-47fe-84ec-77eb-b0a1-5532-09ce
3. Download the audio book from your e|LIVE digital locker and begin enjoying your new digital entertainment package today!